Gray Feather's Fog

Jo Hammers

Gray Feather's Fog

Table of Contents

Gray Feather's Fog

Jo Hammers

CHAPTER ONE

DUMPING A BRIDE

Christmas Eve wedding was about to begin in a small town in Texas called Bullhorn. Dr. Ralph Archer, the groom, stood in the minister's office just off the altar area dressing and looking at his reflection in a mirror that was hung by the door. He was in shock at what his bride had chosen for him to wear. Since they lived across country from each other, she had made all of the wedding decisions. They flew back and forth meeting in motel rooms for weekends of hot romance and not getting to really know each other. They had met in Hawaii when they both were vacationing. She was from Texas and he was from New Jersey. Until now, he never realized that she had such awful taste.

"I can't wear this ridiculous outfit." He muttered to himself shaking his head. He had taken his jeans, T-shirt, and tennis shoes to put on the wedding outfit his fiancé had chosen for him. He stood barefoot looking in the minister's office mirror. He was in total shock.

Before making their way to the church to dress, he and his best friend Doctor Michael Haven, dressed casually in jeans and T-shirts, had been looking at horse trailers. They needed a new one for their veterinarian clinic back in New Jersey. A horse trailer was the equivalent of an ambulance for sick, large animals. They had taken advantage of the morning free of wedding obligations to purchase one and have it shipped.

Having discarded his jeans and tennis shoes, Ralph Archer stood in his appointed long white polyester angel robe with two small wings stitched on the back. He stared into the mirror next to the entry door to the room he and his best man were dressing in. In his opinion, he had to be dreaming and experiencing a pre-wedding nightmare. His wedding garment looked like a cheap New Year's Eve party costume that some Aunt Bessie had made without her glasses on.

Doctor Michael Haven, his best man who had flew in from New Jersey, was snorting and equally as shocked looking at the best man's angel frock that was identical to the groom's. He had also discarded his jeans and tennis shoes and was standing barefoot in shock. Looking over Ralph's shoulder into the mirror he broke out in a snort.

"Connie expects us to wear these? We look like flying targets for some red neck hunter?" His best man stated in a disgusted voice shaking his head. "If she wanted us to be angels, why didn't she at least let us be respectable ones wearing white tuxedos and huge fake wings from a costume shop?"

"I look like a poorly dressed Christmas angel who has gone out and rocked a goose to death for its wings." Doctor Ralph Archer the groom replied. "I honestly don't know what Connie was thinking when she had these made?"

"I am not wearing this ridiculous, animal insulting costume, Ralph. This low class, cheap piece of costume crap has to be the most embarrassing thing I have ever been asked to put on. You should have told me about her angel idea ahead of time. This costume is insulting to me as an animal rights activist."

"We look pretty ridiculous, don't we?" Ralph Archer the groom stated to his friend. "I just pinched myself to see if this moment is a bad dream. I had to euthanize a pet goose last week that had been mauled by a dog. I think that goose has come back to haunt me?"

"I am an animal rights activist, Ralph. Wearing decapitated goose wings goes against every animal activist principal that I stand for. Didn't you check out the wedding clothes before today?"

"I honestly thought we would be wearing white tuxedos and maybe angel wing tie tacks." Ralph Archer replied not knowing what to say. He was disgusted with Connie's choice of wedding wear for him and his lifetime friend. He continued to look in the mirror in shock.

Doctor Michael Haven sighed trying to find the words to tell his friend that he was not going to stand up with him in the robe he had on. He didn't buy leather shoes, carry a leather wallet or have a watch with a leather wrist band. He was a vegetarian who picketed inhumane processing plants. Thoughts of the decapitated goose killed for its wings repulsed him.

"I left the wedding plans up to Connie. She had a wedding planner." He stated eyeing his reflection in the mirror and then glancing down at his bare feet peeping out from beneath his white robe. Connie had told him his wedding garment would be waiting for him in the church. He had taken her word that it would be his size and ready to put on. Looking at his reflection in disgust, wedding jitters and second thoughts set in. He began to laugh uncontrollably. "I have goofed up big time, haven't I Michael?"

"If you marry her, there is no getting a divorce Ralph. Don't forget that you are Catholic the same as I.   As a veterinarian and your friend, these winged robes are an insult to you as a conscientious man as well as a physician. I suggest you take the nearest exit and run while you have a chance. If she puts goose wings on you on your wedding day, your children are going to run around in sheep skins for Christmas and with real rabbit ears on their heads at Easter. She killed a pair of innocent geese to get these two sets of wings. Hunters at least eat the meat. I bet she didn't eat the goose meat. It is probably discarded in a taxidermist's trash can. Look out there and see if the bridesmaids have goose wings on their dresses as well?"

Ralph peeped out the door and back to the rear of the church where the bridesmaids were lined up ready to begin the processional. His heart fell into his gut. There hadn't been just two geese killed for his wedding day. He had been an unknowing participant in the mutilation of a flock of geese.

"They have goose wings on their bridesmaid dresses. I must be in an animal activist's hell." Ralph replied suddenly aware that he was marrying an animal abusive fruitcake. He had spent his weekends in bed with her and hadn't got to know who she really was.

"How many bridesmaids are there?" Michael asked looking over Ralph's shoulder.

"There are six plus the maid of honor." Ralph stated and closed the door and returned to look at his image in the mirror. He was going to be the laughing stock of all his family and friends who had flown in and were now sitting in the sanctuary. Worst than that, he was going to be in trouble with the God of his conscious.

"I didn't see Connie. Is she wearing a pair of goose wings too?" Michael asked in total disgust rolling his tennis shoes, socks, and T-shirt up into his jeans so he could grab them easily if need be. Then he rolled his friend Ralph's clothing and shoes up in the same fashion making two neat little rolls. In the back of his mind, the sensible thing was to make a run for the door. It was two minutes till the processional music started. There wasn't time to change back.

"She said her wings would match mine." Ralph stated staring at himself in disbelief. "I really thought we were going to be wearing matching pieces of costume jewelry in the form of wings."

"These costumes are an insult, Ralph. We are vegetarians as well as vets. How can you justify her killing ten or more geese just so she can have wings for this wedding? We save animals, not kill them for their feathers." Dr. Michael Haven spewed.

Ralph looked one more time into the mirror in disbelief. Then a knock sounded at the door startling the two doctors who thought it was the cue for them to take their places in the front of the church so the wedding could begin. The door opened and Ralph's future father- in- law, Pete Carlson, stuck his head in.

"Don't you boys look great? I shot those geese myself and sent the wings to a taxidermist to have them for today. My little Connie wanted real feathered angel wings for her wedding and she has them. You are one lucky man, Ralph. You didn't even have to waste your bullets killing the geese. You have a future father-in-law that comes thru when needed. Next month, I want you to go hunting with me and the boys. We will shoot a wild boar, roast him, and have a beer bust with the other hunters afterwards. It will give you something to look forward to. Bring your buddy there. "

"I will remember." Ralph replied not knowing what to say. Suddenly his whole reason for marrying Connie Carlson flashed before his face. A life of hot sex with a bikini beauty was suddenly not a priority. Connie's redneck, Texas family were not vegetarians or keepers and protectors of the planet. Michael was right. He didn't want his future children to grown up killing geese for wings, eating wild hogs, or wearing real sheep skins in holiday plays.

"Two minutes and here comes the bride!" Pete Carlson stated grinning from ear to ear.

"I have got to have a little strong nip of something. I have the jitters."Ralph stated suddenly feeling flushed and nauseated.

"Here," said his father-in- law to be pulling a flask from his pocket. Both you boys have a little nip and I will get it back after the service. I have got to go claim my position next to your goose winged bride."

"Thank you sir," stated Ralph.

Pete Carlson owned twenty-five hundred acres of Texas ranch country as well as the local meat packing and processing plant. After handing Ralph his flask of whiskey, he withdrew his head from the dressing room door and closed it.

Ralph turned to his best man big eyed and white as a sheet. "You are right, Michael. I cannot marry her. Where is the nearest exit?"

"Well pal, there is only one way out of here. We are going to walk normally half way across the front of the church. We will then turn and when I say go, fly like hell down the center aisle. The front door is the nearest exit out. Fly fast and don't look back. Pray that your redneck father-in-law to be isn't packing a weapon."Doctor Michael Haven the best man replied grabbing his roll of clothes and those of Ralph. He then stuffed them up under his robe. Hopefully, everyone would assume he had a rather large beer belly.

The wedding music started. They would have to make a run for it in their angel robes with gray goose wings. Michael put his arms beneath the two bundles holding them in place beneath the front of the robe he was wearing. He looked like a pregnant male angel. Although, he was considered a New Jersey stud, his new look didn't matter. He was saving his friend from a disastrous marriage. Ralph was like a brother to him and always had been.

"Lead the way!" Ralph stated his color and common sense returning to him. His adrenaline started to kick in."I am not getting married in goose wings for any woman. We are out of here."

"Why did you ask her to marry you to begin with?" Michael inquired shuffling the load beneath his robe to secure it.

"She looked great in a bikini and the weekends with her were hot. The fact she is worth seventeen million is nothing to laugh at."

"The wedding march is playing, Ralph. Walk slowly to the center of the church where the minister is standing waiting on us. we are going to have to run past the bridesmaids walking towards us. When I say go for it, run and don't look back. My red rental car is around the corner to your right. Here are the keys. I will run the opposite direction yelling insults at them and they will chase me giving you a chance to escape. I will call a Taxi at the convenience store we passed on the way to the church. My billfold is in my jeans and I will meet you at the motel after I ditch anyone following me."

"I feel like such a jackass standing her up."

"Write her a 'Dear John' note after we are back in New Jersey telling her you are an animal activist and couldn't in good conscience condone her killing of a flock of birds for their feathers. You owe it to the ten dead geese to drop her winged ass."

The two doctors in their late twenties opened the door and peeped out. There were at least four hundred guests sitting and waiting for them to take their positions. The bride's maids were in line at the back door getting ready to start as soon as they received the signal from the minister.

"You follow me and walk to the center of the altar area and face the minister.

11

Act like nothing is wrong. Turn when I do and then run like Hell down the center aisle!" Michael whispered. "I will be right behind you and run defense holding back anyone who might try to tackle, trip, or catch you. I have got your backside."

"I owe you one for bringing me to my senses! Do you want me to save you at the altar from Jennifer anytime soon?"

"We will talk about that when we get home to New Jersey. Right now, it is time to spread our goose wings and fly."

Taking a deep breath, Michael opened the door and stepped out into the front of the church. He smiled and gave a little sheepish grin at the crowd of wedding guests as he walked big bellied toward the center front of the church and stood in front of the minister. Ralph, adrenaline flowing, suddenly regained his wits and his sense of humor kicked in as he followed Michael out. Stopping a little short of the center of the church, he suddenly did a couple airplane turns like a little kid. He flapped his arms up and down in his white robe pretending to fly. The crowd broke out into good natured wedding day laughter. Ralph then made an extra turn or two pretending to fly for some children who were sitting on the second row. They giggled and sat up straight to watch. After getting the attention of everyone with his flying maneuvers, he took his position in front of the minister. The crowed was snickering and snapping cameras. He was definitely a hit with the crowd.

"Hamming it up a little?" Michael asked in a whisper as Ralph flew in and landed next to him continuing to flap his wings. "Get ready."

Whistles and laughter was ensuing from the crowd. They loved the Christmas Eve groom who took the time to fly and show off his wedding garment. A cousin of Ralph who was still hung over from the previous night bachelor party yelled, "Where are your angel pants, Ralph? Did the stripper keep them?"

Ralph blushed, waved at his cousin, and then stood still next to Michael waiting for his cue.

"Fly Angel fly!" Michael suddenly yelled.

Ralph ran like crazy down the center aisle. A confused but excited crowd scrambled to their feet to see what was happening. Perhaps he was going to fly to the back relieving Pete Carlson of Connie and then the two of them fly together to the altar. What they didn't expect, was Michael running slower holding his mid section running interference for Ralph. With one hand he waved at the laughing guests of whom many were Ralph's relatives and friends that he knew. He wasted no time in his own flight down the center of the aisle. Connie Carlson's mouth was wide open. He stopped and quickly grabbed one of her goose wings and pulled it from her wedding gown with his one free hand with her screaming. "That is for the geese!" he yelled avoiding the grabbing hands of a couple of Pete Carlson's men.

"Is this some weird part of your wedding that I haven't been told about?" Pete Carlson asked Connie thinking that Ralph and Michael would fly back thru the doors and fly her up to the altar with them. Connie had always been nuts in the way she did things. She didn't answer. She was in shock thinking Ralph was pulling some odd ball prank before their vows.

The wedding photographer jumped up on a pew with his cameral rolling. Wedding guests grabbed cameras to snap pictures of the fleeing groom and best man. It was freaky, but the pair of doctors from New Jersey stole the show. The bride was upstaged in a big way.

"Don't look back, run!"Michael shouted as they flung open the church door and exited."Pete Carlson has pulled out a hand gun."

As Pete Carlson suddenly headed for the door, the musical program for the wedding got mixed up and the soloist started to sing a pop song called SPREAD YOUR WINGS AND FLY which was the bride's choice of solo to be sung after their vows. The crowd broke out into laughter. A three hundred pounds or more huge obese woman, who was apparently having an attack of asthma from the excitement, shuffled out of the chapel pushing bridesmaid and guests out of her way. No one paid her any attention. The crying mad, cursing bride had their attention. It was a Christmas Eve wedding that would be remembered and talked about for years. The photographer's footage of the fleeing angels would be seen nationally. Doctor Michael Haven, the best man, would become famous for the event.

The dumping of wealthy Connie Carlson at the altar was the most exciting thing that had happened in Bullhorn, Texas since Pete Carlson's third wife ran off with the supervisor from the Carlson Processing Plant in a semi truck and took a trailer load of beef cattle with her across the border into Mexico. Half of the wedding guests secretly hated the Carlson family. They had money, seventeen million, but they were rednecks and ruthlessly mean.

What sounded like gun shots permeated the air silencing the crowd of wedding guests. People pushed and shoved trying to get out of the church to see the rest of the wedding madness and possibly Pete Carlson shoot his daughter's groom to death in front of the church. Everyone who lived in the area of Bullhorn, Texas knew he was capable of it. There were whispers that his third wife was possibly dead and buried in the dessert somewhere. No one had heard from her since she supposedly ran off.

Outside, Ralph bolted flew down the church steps not looking back. He heard what he thought was a gun shot behind him. He wasted no time sprinting around the corner and unlocking his friend's red rental car, opening the door, sliding into the seat, and squealing the tires pulling out. Hearing gunshots behind him, he knew he was dead meat and on his way to Pete Carlson's processing plant to be ground up into dog food. He didn't look back.

Meanwhile, seeing his friend run around the corner heading for the red rental car, Doctor Michael Haven sprinted in the opposite direction stopping briefly to wave at the crowed spilling out on to the church's steps. His intention was to keep the crowd looking at him while his friend Ralph, the groom, was making his escape in the opposite direction. He waved his free arm up and down mimicking the way Ralph flew up front in the church before they made a quick exit. He had the spilling out crowd's attention. Then he heard what sounded like gun shots and he ran down a side street to get out of sight fearing that Pete Carlson was shooting live ammo at him. Instantly, he had one goal, to find a quick place to change from the white goose winged robe and into his jeans and tennis shoes. He had his billfold and cell phone in his jeans pocket. He would have no problem catching a taxi out to the motel where he and Ralph were staying.

Darting down a side street, he spotted a rental moving van about half way down the block parked along the curb with its back door rolled up. It looked half loaded. He ran and jumped up in the back to hide for a moment and change out of the ridiculous angel's robe. Standing in the rear where it was about a third empty, he let the two rolls of clothing and shoes drop out from beneath the robe he was wearing. He was barefoot having put no shoes or sandals on with the angel robe in the church. He jerked the robe up and reached for a pair of the jeans sticking one leg in and then the other. Pulling them up, he realized that they were Ralph's and not his. He checked the pocket to see if Ralph's cell phone was available in the pocket to call a taxi with. Ralph's jean pockets had nothing in them except a couple one dollar bills and a small amount of change. He decided to get rid of the goose winged robe and started pulling it up in preparation to pull it off over his head. He was about to pull it over his head when the truck lurched forward throwing him tumbling head first out of the truck. With arms tied up in the robe and his face covered, he fell hard. He hit the pavement rolling. His and Ralph's possessions remained in the back of the moving van which was moving down the street with the back door rolled up.

Three blocks down the street, the driver realized his back door was up, got out, and pulled the roll door down, not seeing the small pile of unfamiliar clothing.

Dr. Michael Haven was stunned as he sat up in the center of the city street. He immediately put both of his hands on the sides of his head and held it rocking. The world was spinning and he felt stunned. Unable to comprehend what had happened to him, he sat in the middle of a residential neighborhood street with cars honking and going around him. Thinking he was drunk, a couple of irate drivers yelled for him to get out of the road. Anyone not knowing the story of the wedding and the robe saw him sitting there as some sort of Christmas Eve drunken fruitcake who had tied one on early in the evening.

The good looking twenty-eight year old veterinarian and animal activist sat in the middle of the street barefoot wearing an angel robe and jeans. He had no ID on him or anything that said he was a successful doctor from New Jersey. He looked like a drunk that had wandered off from a cross dresser's Christmas costume party. His one oddity was that his hair was nicely braided down his back with a feather attached. Destiny set a series of events in to motion charting a new path for Dr. Michael Haven's life. He would, before the day was over, become Gray Feather the medicine man to a Weelo Indian tribe.

Both of the young twenty eight year old doctors from New Jersey escaped the Carlson's and their wedding madness. However, they couldn't escape fate.

CHAPTER TWO

LOST IN A FOG

I talian heritage Doctor Michael Haven was an extremely handsome man. He had jet black waist length hair that had been braided for the Texas wedding of his long time friend Dr. Ralph Archer. Going western for the weekend had been his friend Ralph's idea. Michael had actually thought the fake gray feather and beads in his hair looked pretty ridiculous. In New Jersey, twenty-eight year old Michael Haven was an animal doctor by day and a hard rock musician playing the guitar in clubs at night. Steak eating ranchers, wild animal's horns on walls, feathers, and barbecue wild boar were definitely not his thing. His friend Ralph had asked him to have his rocker's hair braided for the wedding and a feather added for the Texas barbecue reception that the bride had planned afterwards. He had agreed to be his friend's best man, but wasn't happy about the barbecue idea. He was a vegetarian, veterinarian and an animal rights activist.

Now, Doctor Michael Haven sat on the ground in the middle of a busy city street in Bullhorn, Texas in a dazed condition. Cars were whizzing by driving in the wrong lane honking for the drunk in the street to get out of the road. He was too confused to comprehend where he was or the need for him to move.

A couple minutes passed by. The rental truck was long gone that he had fallen out of. An old rusted, pea green, beat up Cadillac stopped in the middle of the side street forcing cars to go around and protecting the man in a white robe from getting hit. A huge Indian woman, weighing at least three hundred and fifty pounds, exited the car and laboriously walked to where the angel robed man sat to see what the problem was. There was a smile on her face saying that she had won the lottery. She waved stranger's cars on past as she made her way to the side of the man that she knew was the groom who had dumped her half sister.

Pansy Sky Walker was a half blood Weelo Indian and her socialite sister named Connie Carlson hated her guts and had snubbed her for years. Not receiving a wedding invitation was the worst. She had crashed the wedding intending to stand and make a scene when the minister asked if there was any reason why the bride and groom shouldn't be joined. Her sister was a lesbian and she had intended to tell the whole world her sister's closeted secret and embarrass the hell out of her. Now, here sat Connie's socially acceptable doctor from New Jersey in the middle of the street needing help. It didn't get any better than that. What she didn't know was that he was the best man, not the groom. The pair of Italian men looked a lot alike and had been dressed in identical angel robes.

Michael looked up briefly and saw a very obese girl in her early twenties standing in front of him in a long purple skirt and moccasins. She weighed at least three hundred and fifty pounds and was laboring to breathe. It was evident that her obesity was going to kill her. He didn't know why he knew that her health was in such bad condition. He just knew.

"What are you doing sitting in the middle of the road, medicine man?" asked the girl who eyed the fake gray feather in the back of his braid as well as the goose wings on the back of his white robe. She was having trouble stooping to check on him. Her extreme overweight was making it difficult to bend.

"I am not sure. Do I know you?" he asked holding his head. He had a terrible throbbing headache.

"Yes, I know you! You are the new medicine man for the Weelo tribe. I have been looking for you. Are you drunk?"

"Apparently so," he replied holding his head."I can't remember my name or what bar I have wandered away from. "

"Give me your arm and I will help you up. I saw you fall. Grandmother Moon Dance sent me to find you."

"Who is Grandmother Moon Dance? "

"She is our leader, you drunken piece of Indian crap." She replied loving her piece of good fortune.

"I have a band leader and her name is Moon Dance? What club does she play in?" he asked and then wondered why he had insinuated his grandmother was a bar lowlife.

"I was parked down the street looking for you." She lied. She was taking him home with her and had every intention of taking advantage of him while he was confused. She was going to toy with Connie's groom and later throw it in her face.

"You were looking for me," he asked in a state of confusion.

"It isn't the first time. You should know better than to go drinking with the young bucks. You are aging, Gray Feather, and you just can't hold your liquor anymore."

"I am a drunk and my name is Gray Feather?" he asked holding his head that was throbbing.

"We must go before the crazy people back at the church see you." She stated putting her ample arm underneath his arm pit and helping him up and then steadying him.

"The church has crazy people in it . . . ?" he asked from his fog.

"It is Christmas. White men put on manger scene plays with angels like you hired to stand out in the cold freezing your touché off. How much did they pay you, Gray Feather, to wear that ridiculous robe and where is your pay?"

"I am a white man's hired Christmas angel?"

"You are not the only one. Your friend, who was also dressed like an angel, ran like hell and left you with one of the Carlson boys taking a pot shot at you. What did the two of you do, rip off the minister's offering box or drank the communion wine?"

"I have a friend and we stole from the church?" he asked totally confused taking his hands down from the sides of his forehead. Then he glanced down at the robe he was wearing over jeans. His feet were bare and sticking out the bottom legs of jeans. Then he fingered the braid that was hanging over his shoulder and fingered the unfamiliar beads and fake gray feather. Unable to comprehend his situation due to his head injury, he let the girl help him to her car.

After helping him in the passenger side, she shuffled slowly around to the driver's side of the old rusted convertible, got in, and started the engine.

"You have been hitting the whiskey bottle again, medicine man? How about a strong cup of coffee to help you sober up?"

"I am on one hell of a drunk. My head is spinning and I may need to throw up," he replied closing his eyes and trying to control his nausea.

"We will swing thru Mc Dees for coffee and soda."

The throbbing in Michael's head started to ease up a tiny bit, so he turned his face and looked at the overweight girl in a deep confusion as to who she was as well as himself. In spite of being in drunken hangover misery, his heart fluttered seeing what beautiful dark brown eyes she had as well as pronounced dimples.

18

He was a sucker for dimples. "Who am I and who did you say you were?"

"Your name is Gray Feather." She replied grinning and looking at the fake gray feather attached to his braid. It was good as any name her Indian friends had. "My name is Pansy Sky Walker."

"Gray Feather?" he mumbled and then looked at his bare feet and saw that he had jeans on underneath the white robe he wore. He pulled the robe up and checked the jeans for a wallet or anything of a personal nature. There were a couple of one dollar bills and a little change in one of the pockets and that was it. He took another look at the extremely overweight Indian girl and asked, "Why don't I have a billfold?"

"You don't have a lick of sense when you are drunk, Gray Feather. Some cheap tramp from a white man's bar somewhere probably has it and your money is probably long gone."

"Oh . . ." he replied.

Pansy turned off the street and into a fast food drive thru lane. Michael tried desperately to remember who in the hell she was. He could not recall anything about her. He then tried to remember why he had on angel clothes and real wings. As hard as he tried, he was in a total brain fog. He was glad she knew him because he was so drunk and hung over that he couldn't remember his middle name, how old he was, or his birthday. He watched as Pansy Sky Walker paid the fast food girl for coffee and a cold drink.

"I must have tied a good one on last night, Pansy. You did say your name was Pansy, didn't you? "He stated taking the hot coffee from her.

"Indian men shouldn't drink. They don't know when to quit and end up on drunks they can't sleep off. You are a medicine man and should know better." She replied scolding him and secretly loving his confusion thinking he had probably downed a flask of whiskey with her dad just before the wedding started. Pete Carlson was notorious for carrying a flask of whiskey or moonshine on him."

"I will never drink again, believe me," he replied taking off the lid of the coffee cup and blowing the black brew to cool it. He had no recollection of who he was or why he was wearing jeans with only two dollars in the pocket. Perhaps the coffee would bring him back to his senses. He was sure that he was in a bar last night, he just didn't know where. He seemed to remember some stripper doing lap dances."

"You are going to need more than black coffee when grandmother Moon Dance gets a hold of you. You are likely to find your weekend bottle wrapped around your ears. You have only been her assistant a few weeks."

"Assistant . . . I am an assistant?"

"You are a medicine man sent to us from our north tribe up by the Canadian line. If we had known you were a drunk we would have sent you back before accepting you into our tribe. You must straighten up your drunken Indian ass, Gray Feather. Our medicine man, Grandfather Night Shadow, is a little off in his thinking lately. You are his replacement and we need you."

"I am a replacement for Grandfather Night Shadow, a medicine man?"

"Yes, you are our medicine man's replacement. Grandfather Night Shadow is eighty some. You have got to do a serious reality check and figure out what is important. Weekend drunks and three day hangovers afterwards is not living in the real world."

"I'm a man who does not live in reality and answers to a woman named Grandmother Moon Dance?"

"We all answer to her. She is the head of the Weelo tribe till the men choose a new chief. Ours died about six months ago. You are a younger medicine man and you answer to her. You are her assistant. Now, suck it up. This isn't the first bad drunk you have been on. Last week, I pulled you out of a drunken cheap motel party in Las Vegas. I have put off asking you if you are a she-he. Your friends at the party in Las Vegas were definitely gay."

"Holy mother of God, I am Catholic, doomed, and on my way to hell," He replied in a shocked voice and then asked, "I'm gay?"

"The men in Vegas were cross dressers. What do you have on?"

Michael inspected the white angel robe he was wearing. "You won't tell will you?"

"The Weelo tribe is okay with members being different. We have a tribe member named three toes who has two extra big toes which is two males hanging out of his body. Three male spirits were scared by Kachina and jumped into one unborn human body. Three Toes is okay with us except for that fact that the three men in him all love different women. Sometimes Kachina jump out and scare a girl Spirit just as she is about to jump into a newly conceived baby's body. If the girl spirit jumps wrong, she could end up in a male baby that hasn't been born yet. You are one of them. I feel you must be a girl spirit in a male body. It is okay with us if you are a she-he."

"I am a she-he and it is okay if I am a Catholic she-he with the tribe?"

"You converted to being Catholic last week. It is okay. Food pantries expect that sometimes. You hit their food pantry last week for a Christmas charity basket."

"I am an Indian Catholic convert who takes charity?"

"The Weelo are plagued with white men coming to the reservation trying to convert us to their many religions. You converted for food. We all have at one time or another. Sometimes it gets us free shoes or educations. It is easy to convert back. You can embrace the Weelo religion again when you are ready."

"That clears up the religion thing for me. I am Weelo as well as Catholic."

"You are a Weelo medicine man who has been brainwashed in the white man's religious ideas. Our tribe is used to being brainwashed into new religions. The grandmother and grandfather believe a big ship is coming for them like Noah's Ark, the white men's Bible fairy tale." She replied totally loving the brainwashing she was pulling on her sister's run away groom. She hoped his brain fog lasted till she had slept with him. She would love to rub that into her snobby sister's face, especially if she could manage it today on her sister's suppose to be wedding day.

"Thank you for rescuing me! I promise to pay back the church every cent of the stolen offering and the price of the holy wine. What in the world was I thinking?" he replied."I always heard that God would curse you if you drank the Holy Communion unworthy. He has given me one of the worst headaches and drunken fogs that I have ever had and made a believer out of me!"

"That is good. Maybe Grandmother Moon Dance can get some decent work out of you, now that you have made the decision to abstain from whiskey."

"I am one reformed Indian man who will never drink again. If you had my horrific headache, you would give up alcohol to." He stated unsure of who he as Gray Feather was or where he was going. He decided to just let her drive and do her thing till he sobered up.

"Don't expect sympathy from me. Suck it up till you sober up tomorrow." She replied.

"You are an uncaring woman, Pansy Sky Walker." He stated eyeing her. She was big, cuddly, panting, and begging for attention. He liked stray dogs with big brown eyes. They appreciated love and a serious bowl of dog food.

Gray Feather then leaned his head back on the seat and dozed off.

CHAPTER THREE

TRAINING WHEELS

Michael Haven, now renamed Gray Feather, woke up from an hour or so of sleep in the passenger seat of Pansy Sky Walker's old green Cadillac. He had a serious ache in the middle of his upper back from sleeping on the two stiff goose wings on his back. He still was in a brain fog and not thinking clearly.

"My wings are killing me," he stated glancing over at the driver who was smoking a cigarette.

"My weight is killing me." She retorted refusing to show sympathy.

He looked once more down at himself and the angel robe he had on and then felt of the swollen lump on his head. He wasn't sure whether he felt better after dozing or worse. Glancing over at Pansy, he asked, "Am I a dead medicine man who has gone to the other side and has been given his angels wings?" He asked with a serious look on his face stretching as best he could in the passenger seat.

"You could be right, Gray Feather. You could be a dead Weelo Indian who has been awarded his Christmas wings. Do you feel like a Weelo Indian angel?" she asked laughing on the inside sure that her father Pete Carlson had slipped the groom, Gray Feather, a flask of his moonshine just before the wedding was to begin. The rotten moonshine might have been what made the two angels fly and dump the bride.

"You don't understand," he retorted. "I am seriously injured. My angel wings are broken and they are killing me. I have a serious backache to go with my headache. I need you to take a look at the center of my shoulder blades and tell me what is wrong. I could die from broken untreated wings. Birds die every day from being eaten by cats after they break wings and can't fly to safety."

Pansy broke out into hysterical laughter wiping her wet eyes on a couple napkins the fast food drive thru girl had given her earlier. When she was able to keep a straight face she reached over and patted him on the top of his leg in an effort to console her winged angel of a medicine man.

"I apologize for my lack of empathy. Your wings were broken and flopping when you got in my car after your fall. You probably broke them in a bar fight last night. I am taking you home to our medicine woman for treatment. She will get rid of your wings and your halo." She replied loving the crazy fog Gray Feather was in.

"That is just my luck. I need a surgeon and have to settle for an herb doctor."

"Little wings are like the training wheels on a child's bike, Gray Feather. You are a big boy now. You don't need training wings." She replied trying desperately to control her laughter. He was so drunk and so serious."

"I have little broken training wings?" he asked twisting his neck trying to look at his back. He took his suntanned hand and reached over his shoulder feeling and trying to determine his injuries. Then he cried. "Oh God, I have broken my training wings. There probably isn't a decent vet that treats birds for a thousand miles."

Once again, Pansy couldn't control herself and she broke out laughing and snorting. She liked Connie's choice for a husband. However, he was her man now. Her heart was running like a deer when she looked at him. He was a stud and she hated the idea of how many times Connie had slept with him. She was, for some reason, feeling very territorial about him.

"Don't get excited. I will take a look at your broken training wings when we stop in a few minutes to stretch our legs. I will jerk them off and save you a vet bill." She replied biting her lip."After today you will have to walk. Your training wings are history."

"I have to walk? Why? I am sure I have a yellow mustang somewhere."

"Till you remember where you left that horse, you will either walk or ride with me. This old Cad can fly when she wants to. You won't miss your wings or your yellow hay burner horse. My green Cad has enough horsepower to keep us flying."

"Do we live in the dessert?" he asked looking out of the car window. The throbbing in his head earlier had been so extreme that he hadn't paid any attention to the landscape.

"You are a Weelo medicine man and yes, you live in the desert. If you get over this drunken hangover by tomorrow night, you and I might sit together at the tribe's campfire. I am okay with you possibly being a she-he. No man is perfect. I won't tell about you being a cross dresser. That will be our little secret as long as you stay out of my clothes."

"Thank you for keeping my secret! Do cross dresser Indian men date women? Your dimples are causing me to think possibly of sleeping with you. However, I am drunk and could be hallucinating about how beautiful you are. Where is this rusted flying green machine taking us?" He asked sticking his right arm out the window and letting the December breeze cool him down. He felt like he was running a fever.

"You and I have been seeing each other ever since you arrived from the North. We are in New Mexico and on our way to Grandmother Moon Dance's lodge. She is the medicine woman of the Weelo tribe and your boss. You will sleep in her lodge tonight if I can sober you up. She doesn't like Indian men who drink. You are a medicine man and should know better."

"I will sleep in the lodge of a Weelo medicine woman?" he asked totally confused about who he was.

"Medicine men stick together and share a lodge. You can have your own lodge, if you choose to marry. However, don't plan on having your own lodge any time soon. You are a non-committer, a runner. You have turned me down three or four times in the last few weeks. I would have married you the first day you arrived. You are the one for me. I don't care how many times your boots have been set outside the door."

"I am Catholic and one shot at getting marriage right is all I get." He replied and then wondered how he knew he was Catholic and why he couldn't remember being an herb doctor."Why does Grandmother Moon Dance need a Catholic medicine man like me for an assistant?"

"It doesn't matter what your religion is. It is your talents as a medicine man that the Weelo are interested in. You are psychic and speak for the Great Spirit"

"You mean that I am a medicine man, fortune telling quack?" he asked putting one of his bare feet upon the dash trying to get comfortable. His head was making him hurt everywhere.

"The Great Spirit gives you visions or signs. Whatever pops into your mind, you speak to our people. Whatever you are seeing or feeling at the moment, tell it. Fortune telling is not hard. The people will read into your words whatever they want it to mean."

"I am a fake, medicine man, fortune teller. Somehow, I have never considered myself to be a dishonest man. It is a shock to find out that I am a con artist. God has taken my mind away for my dishonesty. I am in a fog. The Great Spirit has taken my thinking. Are God and the Great Spirit the same big fellow?"

"Don't worry, I will make sure you say and do all the right things till your brain fog clears. I will explain to our tribe that you have damaged your communication chip connecting you to the Great Mother ship. They believe in a Great Mother ship similar to the white man's Noah's Ark. If ever in doubt as what to say, speak of pairs of animals."

"Am I Noah? I do like animals."

"Yes, you are a Noah type and you have reincarnated over the years and made you way to us from the Great Mother ship. We are waiting for a great rain to come to the dessert. Till then, we keep our animals outdoors. Cages for animals are for traveling, not every day keeping."

"I do seem to recall a huge room of cages with animals in them. I just don't remember where I saw the room."He replied totally confused about being a Noah type.

"How did you get stuck with such small wings, Gray Feather?" Whoever de-signed your angel robe and wings did a poor job. They have no sense of propor-tion. They look like something Connie would throw together to save a buck."

"My wings are too small and Connie designed them for me? Am I married to a Connie?"

"She is just a wing maker and no, you are definitely not married to her. How-ever, I am sure she felt that she would be married to you tonight."

"Does she have a crush or something on me?"

"Forget the wing maker, she isn't your type. Let us get back to the wings. You are going to have to discard your broken wings before they set up an infection or a permanent physical injury to your mid shoulder area."

"Does Connie, the angel wing maker, dwell in the Great ship in the sky?" he asked totally in the dark on anything and everything.

"Of course, she made your wings and robe. However, I think the mother of us all should fire her. She doesn't have much fashion sense in my book. I would have put you in a white tuxedo with holes in the back for your wings. You look pretty pathetic in that poorly made white polyester robe that looks like it was made for a woman to wear, not a man."

"A white tux does seem to make sense to me. Can I ask to have my clothes and wings made by someone other than her?" He asked innocently. He had no memories of his friend Ralph's fiasco of a wedding.

"You won't be issued another pair of wings while on Earth. You will have to fly with me on the reservation in this green cad. You must bury your wings in the dessert, grieve for them, and then walk as a human man till the Great Mother ship comes for us. You are no longer a flying hunk of an angel. You are a green Cadillac rider."

"I am to bury my angel wings, grieve, and then walk for the rest of my Earth life except when I am riding with you?"

"You have got the drift, Gray Feather." She replied reaching over and patting the top of his leg that was nearest her.

"Am I drunk, nuts, or both?" He asked eyeing her dimples which fascinated him. He liked her and was sure he had never dated a large woman before. However, in his brain fog, he was not sure how he knew that he had never dated a plus size woman."

"Grandmother Moon Dance will know how to treat your head fog and your wounded spirit. I hate to tell you this Gray Feather, you are drunk and nuts. You are lucky, I go for crazy."

"Is there any chance that you and I might share a lodge?" he asked thinking about her hand on his leg earlier and how comforting it felt.

"Ask me after you are over your drunken fog."She replied making her dimples grin at him.

"That sounds reasonable. I am drunk and hitting on you. Put me in my place and keep me there till I sober up." He stated and then laughed. "Since I am drunk, I might as well tell you that I think I remember being in love with you. It must be your big brown eyes. Do you have a cold nose?" Then he muttered to himself. "Where did that come from? I made her sound like a dog."

"I will help you get over your drunken fog if you will do something for me, Gray Feather." She stated taking a quick glance at him.

"What do you want?"He asked trying to remember who he was or remember anything prior to his severe headache.

"I have been a fat freak my whole life. Just once I would like to be fairly thin and have a man look at me like I am beautiful. As a medicine man, can you help me lose weight? Juanita says you are a gifted doctor."

"Juanita has informed you that I am a gifted medicine man?"He asked mulling the name Juanita over in his mind. It rang no bells."Who is Juanita?"

"She was your lady friend before me. She dumped you for a tall rich Indian man from another tribe who owns a big ranch and lots of cattle. She told me that she dumped you because you are a loser. She also told me that she was tired of you wearing her clothes."

"Juanita left me because I am a loser and a cross dresser?"

"You have your problems, Gray Feather." She replied wanting so hard to laugh. He was drunk and gullible.

"Was losing Juanita the reason for my drinking binge last night? Did I want to leave you and go home to her?"

"She is history, Gray Feather. Your heart will mend. I am a skinny woman next to her."

Doctor Michael Haven, now Gray Feather, would never be the same when she got thru with him. This was the first chance she had ever had to get even for all the neglect and denial her father had given her. Connie had everything. Now she had what Connie wanted, her groom. If possible, she would get pregnant by Gray Feather. That would be the ultimate knife she could put in Connie and her Father's heart. She knew that Gray Feather, being a successful New Jersey Doctor, would not stick around and love an obese Indian woman with an eighth grade education once his memory returned. She would not let herself fall in love with him. She would just sleep with him.

"I plan to turn over a new leaf, Pansy Sky Walker. I am going to walk the straight and narrow. I am going to be an honest medicine man. I promise to never drink or go to the white men's bars again. Also, I will stay out of your closet and leave your clothes alone. If I am a she-he, I will ask the girl in me to choose another body and jump back out."

Pansy broke out in another round of laughter. "Gray Feather, you are one unique man. I could fall madly in love with you. However, I am not going to let myself. I must help keep you on the straight and narrow."

"I appreciate your support." He stated eyeing her winking dimples.

"If you should choose to sneak out of Grandmother Moon Dance's lodge tonight and find your way to where I sleep, I am agreeable."

"I must turn you down, Pansy Sky Walker. I have a headache."

Jo Hammers

Michael Haven, still feeling a bit out of it, lay his head back on the seat and dozed thinking he needed to sleep off a bad hangover. Somehow, he didn't remember getting drunk or having a taste for alcohol. However, he was an Indian and they sometimes were known for not holding their liquor very well. He was sure that he must have really tied on a good one to be in the brain fog he was in. He had a terrible headache.

As he dozed, he began to dream. He could see all kinds of cats and dogs smiling at him. He dreamed of taking a big container of dog biscuits and cat food morsels off a shelf. Then, he would take handfuls of the treats and toss them up into the air and watch as the animals scrambled with tails wagging to claim a biscuit or morsel. A man in a white robe appeared asking him to help him escape. He ran with the man and then got lost from him. He couldn't figure out why strangers in the dream were snapping cameras and yelling, "Fly, Angel, fly." Then he dreamed of the Indian girl Pansy Sky Walker. She had roving hands that were all over him and then she had her hands around his neck squeezing the life out of him. Also, he saw an older little woman who came to his rescue and made his headache go away. Pansy Sky Walker became a dog and he saw himself walking her over and over and over. Then Pansy the dog turned into a beautiful Indian maiden with long black hair that hung loose to her hips. All the Indian men, who hadn't seen her as desirable up to that point, suddenly wanted her. However, she was his dog and he wanted to keep her. Then he dreamed of Noah's Ark and he was the veterinarian on board."

Pansy's old Cadillac hit a bump in the road as she turned onto a dirt road entering a two hundred acre small ranch known as the Weelo Indian Reservation. Dr. Michael Haven, now Gray Feather the Medicine man woke up. He stretched, yawned, and then flinched from a sore muscle in the center of his shoulders. He cried out in pain. He had fallen asleep with the stiff goose wings behind him and the result was a muscle ache. He ran his fingers across the top of his head and was pleased that his headache was letting up. He blinked his eyes and then rubbed them and yawned. He wasn't sure where he was or what time of the evening it was. The sun was going down. He tried to remember his birthday or age. He still couldn't pull that information up.

"It is about time you rejoined the living, are you hungry? We could kill a rabbit and eat him. I have a camp stove in the trunk."

"I am a vegetarian. I do not eat meat or kill animals." He replied and then wondered how he knew he was a vegetarian.

"The desert isn't plentiful in green things, medicine man."

"Pull over, Pansy Sky Walker. I have got to discard my wings. They are killing me." Gray Feather demanded feeling like he had to stretch and throw away the ridiculous robe he had on. He didn't have a clue why he was wearing it or where he got it.

"Good thinking, Gray Feather. It is time for you to take the form of an ordinary medicine man. The Weelo will not respect a leader who arrives in white men's angel clothing. It is time for you to discard the leftovers of your yesterday life."

Pansy pulled the car to the side of the road in the dessert. Michael Haven, now Gray Feather, got out and pulled the white robe off. He studied briefly the two wings sewn into the back of the garment. In his thinking, the wings looked like goose wings. However, he was an animal lover. He would not dismember a goose just so he could have wings. They had to be broken training wheel wings just as Pansy Sky Walker had said. Perhaps Pansy Sky Walker sewed them back on while he had been asleep in an attempt to help him. She wasn't a surgeon in his thinking, but she had done her best.

Pansy exited the driver's side of the car and joined Gray Feather on the edge of the desert and took a deep breath of the evening air that was cooling down. She had been having trouble breathing all day and had just about overdosed herself on her inhaler. She was relieved to be able to breathe.

"What will I do with my broken, training wheel wings, Pansy? They are dead, decaying, and smell."

"You must return the wings to the Great Goose Spirit and let him do what he wants with them." She replied amused. "You have no use for them in their broken condition. Perhaps you will grow a new set of adult size ones with time. Winged creatures coming to us from the Great Spirit do that sometimes. "

"Should I just discard them like litter? I seem to remember being anti-litter."

"Hold them up to the sky and ask the Great Goose Spirit to take them and give you a sign that it is okay to litter and leave them in his desert."

"To me, the gray wings look similar to those of a Canadian goose. Do you suppose angels and geese are similar in body?"

"Ordinarily Gray Feather, a northern goose angel should be returned to Canada for burial. However, I am too short on gas money to make the trip. We must ask the Great Goose Spirit to take the wings back to the Great Mother ship from here. The white choir robe is a different ball game. Since you converted to being a Catholic, you will have to do white man's penance for it. You have probably stolen it from the church earlier today."

"Since I plan to convert back to being Weelo, maybe I won't need to do penance for the robe. Maybe the Great Spirit will honor my sincere regret over my drunkenness and take the wings and robe back to where they belong. Maybe the Great Spirit will send the Great Goose Spirit to relieve me of both."

Pansy snickered like a little girl that had been totally amused over some stupid little something. Then she let herself consider how wonderful he was. He was childlike and sincere in his brain fog and intentions. She was going to enjoy her time with her sister's groom till his fog went away. She might have a couple days with him before he sobered up. He was extremely handsome and not a man that would have ever looked at her had he not needed her at the moment. She had him at a disadvantage. He didn't remember how wonderful he was. He was ordinary and needy like her. He was her man till he remembered who he was. The longest drunken hangover she remembered one of the Indian men having lasted about three days. She would make the most of the time she had with him. She would have a few days of wonderful memories for once in her life and then rub his infidelity into her sister, Connie's face.

An animal was startled by their sudden presence as the stood on the shoulder of the back road. Pansy and Gray Feather didn't see the big Jack Rabbit sitting quietly near them. They were more interested in getting rid of the stinking goose wings which reeked with the smell of formaldehyde. The rabbit watched them with big eyes as it tried to hide in the shadow of a cactus.

Gray Feather pulled off the robe and stood barefoot and with a bare chest. His tight jeans only enhanced how beautiful his body was. His braided black hair hung down his back with the feather moving in the evening breeze. He looked like he belonged on the front of a book or a calendar of male hunks. There was no mistaking the fact that he was definite eye candy for any woman young or old.

Now that he had removed the wings and robe, Pansy gasped. He was the man she had always dreamed would one day come and love her forever. She suddenly wanted him and not just for a couple of days till his brain fog cleared. Her heart was racing and out of control.

"I am a little hazy as what the words are that I, as a medicine man, should say to or ask of the Great Spirit to take the wings and the robe. Do you have any suggestions?" he asked holding the white robe with sewn on goose wings to the sky in an offering stance.

"Just tell him you are returning the two items and that you are sorry for breaking the wings." She replied. "It is like returning an item to a department store that you have used and it has a spot food on it. Just give the Great Spirit, who is like the store clerk, your best story."

"Great Big Goose Keeper Spirit in the sky. I am returning your wings and thank you for loaning them to me to fly here. I now give them back. They are broken because the woman, Pansy Sky Walker who is standing next to me, didn't rescue me in time to prevent me from falling and breaking them." He stated hoping his ceremony was appropriate and happy with his ritual.

"You just blamed your broken wings on me, Gray Feather. Do you expect the Great Spirit to punish me for your drunkenness?"

"You told me that Grandmother Moon Dance sent you to get me. You were parked on the curb smoking a cigarette when I ran past you. Somehow, I seem to remember that. Your cigarette was more important to you than my safety. You let me fall and sit in the middle of the street till you finished your puffing. You neglected me."

"Pansy Sky Walker eyed the hunk of a man that was cracking her up with his brain fog. She had been sitting along the curb, but it was because she needed a puff or so of her inhaler. It may have looked like a cigarette or a cigar. When he and his best man ran past her in the church with their goose wings flopping, they stirred up dust in the air and set off her Asthma. She had exited the church right after them needing to medicate her lungs. She had driven past this running winged man, turned onto a side street, and parked along the curb. She needed a safe place to sit, inhale her medicine, and wait for her attack to ease up out of sight of her father and sister who would have been irate at her for crashing the wedding. Gray Feather had turned down the same side street and ran past her. She had watched him try to change clothes in the back of the rental van as well as watched him fall out when the van lurched forward pulling away from the curb.

"You are right, Gray Feather. My puffing may have contributed to your head injury. However, I think your reason for falling and bumping your head was a result of your cross dressing. You probably tripped on the hem of that woman's choir robe you have on when you were running from the church."She retorted.

"I am glad we are in agreement, Pansy Sky Walker. I would hate for the Great Spirit to think that I couldn't fly even with training wheels on. It would make me look a little klutzy in his sight. I am sure that all of my friends had their training wings take off long ago. I am a little old for training wings, don't you think? I must be a slow learner."

Pansy laughed and slapped Gray Feather lightly on the back. "Today is the big day, Gray Feather. You are a big boy in the Great Spirit's eyes. Your training wings are history."

"I am glad I have a friend to share this moment with, Pansy Sky Walker."

"Throw the wings and robe into the sky and let the Great Spirit decide what to do with them and we will be on our way." She stated.

Gray feather tossed the robe and wings as high into the sky as he could. The action caught the attention of the Jack Rabbit. Suddenly frightened, it bolted and ran just about the time the robe came down landing on top of it scaring it even more. The robe suddenly had a spirit of its own and moved across the dessert in a zigzag motion with a blind rabbit trying to run out from under it.

Pansy Sky Walker and Gray Feather hadn't seen the rabbit. When the robe hit the ground and then started moving on its own across the dessert, they both screamed and made a run for the old green Cadillac and jumped in.

"That was close!" Gray Feather stated."The Spirit of that goose must have come for his wings. I am glad I was not wearing them. He might have scooped me up and flew me to Canada or Alaska. I will never remove or do surgery on goose wings. You are guaranteed of that." He stated and then wondered why he had used the word surgery. He attributed it to probably having watched too many medical shows.

"Please warn me if you call a spirit from the other side to come from now on. I am not use to medicine men who has actual visits by animal spirits from beyond the grave. You have a gift, Gray Feather, a great gift and I have just now developed a great respect for you. I will play with your knee no more. I do not want to share a bed with a man who can call spirits. I might wake up and find three in the bed instead of just you and me. My weak heart would not be able to handle that. Do all New Jersey doctors have the gift of calling the dead to life?"

"I don't know, Pansy Sky Walker. I have never been to the land of New Jersey or spoken with its doctors that I know of. However, my brain fog has clouded my thinking and remembering."

Pansy bit her lip. She had almost let his identity out. She would have to be more careful.

"Wait till I tell our people about this encounter with the Great Goose spirit. Our stories around the campfires have been a little boring lately and mostly having to do with the hunting of deer. Your Great Goose Spirit will bring new life to our campfire. I will tell of the Goose Spirit that took the white man's angel robe and made it move across the dessert like a sidewinder rattlesnake. The tale will scare the pee out of the tribe elders and the children just like it did me. I am the tribe's story teller."

"You are a story teller?" he asked and was amused that she had admitted to being frightened by the experience in the desert. He was attributing what he had seen to being hung over.

"Yes, I sit with the people of our tribe and tell the stories of our ancestors. I am a walking history book and you are the new story that the Great Spirit has given me to tell. "

"So, you are a writer?"

"No, I am a story teller, a keeper of the history of our people. It is my duty to pass down all the mysteries of the Weelo tribe to our children. When I am gone, one of them will become the keeper of the history of our people. "

CHAPTER FOUR

THE LIGHTS OF HOME

A sudden group of lights appeared in the distance indicating that there was some sort of small encampment of people, although there didn't appear to be any structures. Pansy pulled over to the side of the desert dirt road, switched off the lights, and parked along the edge. Gray Feather surveyed the vast desert, the stars in the early night sky, and the lights from the Weelo tribe's dwellings in the far distance.

"The lights of home are calling, Gray Feather. Are you ready to go face your forgotten memories?"

Gray Feather reached over and took Pansy's hand and held it tightly. Taking a deep breath and biting his lip, he said, "Please help me not to make a fool out of myself till this brain fog lifts and please don't tell my boss, Grandmother Moon Dance, what a drunk I am. She might fire me. I am honestly so hung over that I don't remember any of this."

Pansy glanced over at him as they sat in the old green cad looking at the night sky. For the first time, she saw him as human and felt just a twinge of regret for having brainwashed him all day. Just as quickly, she dismissed her regret thinking of her lifelong desire to get even with Connie. She might never get another chance. For one thing, her health was failing her and she knew it. She might be dead come next year at this time. It was now or never.

"I will be your voice till you regain your thoughts." She replied seeing the frightened lost look on his face. "I won't let you make a fool out of yourself. Just smile and pretend you know everyone and say whatever comes into your mind. The tribe is used to the craziness of medicine men."

"I won't be expected to smoke a peace pipe or offer up live sacrifices, will I? I somehow know that I am a non-smoker as well as a vegetarian."

"No. Nothing will be expected of you. The tribe will see you as a perfect medicine man that refuses the addictions of Earth men. Perfect is good. They will trust you and your words of wisdom. Grandfather Night Shadow drinks on occasion, puffs cigarettes like he is a stove pipe, and looks at the maidens when Grandmother Moon Dance isn't looking. You will gain the respect of our tribe if you avoid the Grandfather's addictions. He reads for the people to feed his habits. If you read just to feed yourself or Grandmother Moon Dance, who often does without because of him, the people will respect you. Her children are all dead except for one daughter, a social worker in town, and a son named Wildcat who is one of our providers. Wild Cat is gone all of the time and there is no one to watch out for her welfare. Her daughter has abandoned the tribe and hasn't been to see Moon Dance in probably six or seven years. The tribe will see you as an honorable man and one who isn't affected by the craziness of Earth life."

"But, I am crazy, Pansy Sky Walker. A man who cannot remember is crazy." He replied.

"Do not tell the people that you cannot remember. I will tell them you have come to us from our other tribe who lives in the north along the Canadian line. Only I will know that you flew down from the sky on training wings. They might not respect a new medicine man who has just graduated from training wheel wings. You tell the people that you are currently speaking to them from a cloud that the Great Mother Ship has hidden you in to protect you. Our fables and tales are held dearly by the older members of the tribe who have a crazy handed down myth they believe in. They think a great a Great Ship will one day come for them. There is no one coming for us but the US Government when they find out we run a trucking company that does not pay taxes or send our children to Earth schools."

"Are we at war with the government? I have heard of wars with the government over the rights to build casinos. My friend and I used to do the casinos in Nevada occasionally." He replied and then wondered where the 'my friend' words came from and when did he make a trip to Nevada?

"There are all types of crazy when you are an Indian. We are not main stream or what the United States wants its citizens to be. My sister and father are white and mainstream. They say I am the crazy one and for me to drop off the end of the Earth and leave them alone. I am indeed crazy, nuts for loving them."

"So, it doesn't matter if I seem a little odd, I am Weelo and it is okay?"

"You have got it. Crazy is revered amongst the Weelo. It means you are not white."

"I am a cloud engulfed medicine man who does not smoke or eat meat and I speak crazy words from the Great Mother ship" he stated firmly practicing for his appointed Weelo rounds. "How does that sound?"

"You are Gray Feather and uniquely crazy in your own fashion. The bad kind of crazy is caused by people. My sister keeps me on the brink of depression, madness, and suicide. I want her and my father to love me. I try to interact with them, but they don't want me or my attempts. They are a crazy from an outside force. I have my craziness called unloved and you have a brain fog. It is okay for us both to be crazy. You help me with my crazy and I will help you with yours. That is the way of the Weelo."

"I think I am going to like being a Weelo medicine man. I like crazy, I think."

"A few years back, Grandfather Night Shadow had a big green lizard crawl beneath his sleeping blanket while he took an afternoon nap. When he woke, he thought a rattlesnake was in bed with him. He jumped up from his sleeping rug scared out of his wits, ran from the lodge, and yelled hysterically that all the mothers of the tribe were to throw away the rattles they amused their babies with. He insisted that the mothers were attracting rattlesnakes to our camp with the shaking of the rattles. Everyone found the incident amusing and laughed when he was not around. However, all the mothers threw away their baby rattles out of respect. Even if you get something wrong and ask the tribe to throw away something like baby rattles, the tribe will still respect you because you are one of our leaders. The chief is head of the Weelo tribe and the medicine man is next. No one would want to be the enemy of the second in line for leader of our tribe. The disrespect might come back to bite them."

"So, as a medicine man, I am actually a leader like a white man's city mayor or a councilman?"

"Yes, only you are respected. There will be no newspaper articles digging up dirt about whom you once slept with or whether you paid your taxes or took bribes. It is okay with us to take bribes. Recently, I gave Grandfather Night Shadow a carton of cigarettes to inquire of the Great Spirit what to do about my sister who is continually doing hateful things to me. His usual fee is one pack of the puffers. I bribed him at two in the morning to wake up the Great Spirit from his bed and give me an answer. Great Spirits do not like to be waked. Mountains will sometimes rumble or spew forth lava. Grandfather Night Shadow would have to answer for waking him up and wasn't agreeable to do so in the middle of the night. So, I bribed him."

"You dared to wake up God during his time of rest?" Gray Feather asked laughing. He loved the things she came up with. He was sure that there were great interesting stories about the Weelo he couldn't remember. He also wondered if he had ever been bribed to wake up the big man for some reason. He was sure that the Great Spirit had to be Catholic. He seemed to have a minor flash of watching a priest doze off in some kind of booth while he was saying he was sorry for stepping on a bug somewhere.

"I dared, bribed, and got my answer. Only three stars fell from the sky that night. Grandfather Night Shadow said they were three arrows of the Great Spirit shot toward me and him on Earth. He said we were lucky that the Great Spirit was sleepy and his aim was bad."

"What did you ask that couldn't wait for daylight and required a bribe?" He asked.

"I found out my sister was getting married the next day and had not invited me. She was having a huge wedding with many guests and I was slighted as I always am. I was really upset about it. I wanted revenge and needed a quick answer and help. So, I bribed Grandfather Night Shadow and we woke up the Great One who sometimes thunders and sends great winds."

"What did the Great Spirit tell you to do?" Gray Feather asked amused.

"He told me to sit on the back row at my sister's wedding, steal her groom, and make her beg for him back." She replied simply.

"Did you accomplish that act?" he asked laughing. "

Yes, I have him. However, I have a problem. I don't want to give him back. He makes my heart race.

"You can never keep what is not yours to have, Pansy Sky Walker. You must give him back to her."

"No . . . I am going to keep him. My sister has always made me squirm and feel less than her. I will keep her man and use him all up. Revenge will be sweet. I will suck up everything that is sweet about him. He will not be the same when I am thru with him. He will be all used up as a man."

"Revenge is not a good thing, Pansy Sky Walker. Sometimes it comes back and bites you in the butt like a vicious wild dog with a bad set of doggie dentures." He replied and wondered why he was always relating everything to dogs and cats.

"Karma will have to hurry if it bites me in the butt. Unless I lose two hundred pounds, the white doctor I saw last week says I might have a year or so to live. Assisting you as a medicine man may be the last thing I do. I will keep my sister's man and take my chances with the wild dog."

"I was hoping that you were unattached. I find you quite comforting Pansy Sky Walker. You are like a big yellow Collie dog with brown eyes and a cold nose. Should you return your sister's man, I might be interested in you using me all up." He replied grinning.

"I will keep that in mind, Gray Feather. However, I am not a big, cold nosed Collie dog."

"As a medicine man, I plan to help you lose weight and regain your health. You will be my special dog patient." He stated and then was embarrassed that he had called her a dog. He didn't know where those words came from.

"I am sorry that you see me as a dog and not a woman, Gray Feather. I am a half breed and my tribe treats me like I am a wild stray dog. My father and sister have always treated me like I am a mad, rabid dog. I hoped you would see me differently. You are like them with your words." She retorted with a hurt sound in her voice.

Gray Feather was almost afraid to speak with her any further because of the disrespectful words that slipped from his mouth. After a few minutes, he changed the subject and tried to start a new conversation.

"What is my job as a medicine man? Do I have patients or do I just dance around a campfire at a certain time of the month and invoke spirits like the one of the Goose?"

"You will sit outside the lodge of Grandmother Moon Dance on a rug with a little rug next to you. When one of the tribe needs advice, they will come and sit down next to you and cross their legs Indian fashion. They will not speak till you do. The medicine man thinks for a few moments and then asks his rug sitter what he would like to ask of the Great Spirit. You listen and then give your opinion or say whatever comes into your mind. The tribe will take your words and each put their own spin on what you say. You do not interpret the words you give them unless you are in the mood to do so. You just carry messages from the Great Spirit. You are like a mail man. He doesn't read the mail, he just delivers it."

"I am an Indian Medicine Man mail deliverer. . . I get it! Thank you Pansy Sky Walker. "My role as a medicine man is clear to me now. I believe I can function with or without my memories."

Pansy looked at him solemnly and wanted to just let her heart run like a deer and fall madly in love with him. She hated her sister Connie for being beautiful, rich, and having had him.

"You will be a Great Medicine Man. You have that inner and outer something that people love. I do not have that. My inner and outer something is not loved by people. You will do fine and live many years. I will continue to be a woman of disrespect and die with no one caring."She replied.

"I am sorry, Pansy Sky Walker for my words that seem to come out wrong. I will help you lose weight. I promise. I am a good dog doctor." he stated and then bit his lip. He had used the dog word again.

"The psychiatrist, in the white man's hospital, says I eat because I feel unloved. It will take another human to love me to cure my weight problem. I am not a dog, Gray Feather. I do not need your disrespect. To be loved as a dog, is not the love I look for."

"Loving and walking you like a dog is the answer to your weight problem, Pansy Sky Walker."

As soon as the words were out of his mouth, he realized he had once more referred to her as a dog. He saw her flinch. He was not putting his best foot forward. To the contrary, he was alienating Pansy Sky Walker.

"I understand you are making it clear to me that you see me as a dog. You do not have to keep repeating yourself. "

"You don't know how sorry I am over my mouth. I like you and need you Pansy. I am afraid to face the tribe alone in my brain fog. Would you let me be your dog?"

"I will help you till you can function without your memories. However, I am turning you down as a friend and a doctor to treat my obesity. Also, I don't want or need a dog."

"The night air is starting to get to this bad dog. Being barefoot and bare-chested is getting to me. Do I have any clothes on the reservation?" he stated looking at the jeans he had on that somehow he knew weren't his. "

"I will find you some moccasins and a leather vest when we reach the grandmother's lodge. I will make sure that you are safe and have what you need to survive till your brain fog is gone." She stated with a face that read she saw him as an asshole like everyone else in her life.

"I appreciate your offer, Pansy Sky Walker, but I am an animal lover. I will not skin an animal just so I can have shoes or a vest. I will go barefoot and shirtless till I can find clothing that doesn't come from innocent animals. You saw what happened when I tried to give the goose its wings back."

"Good Point," she replied."We are Indians, however, and we live off the land and what it produces. We wear leather clothing and moccasins. You may go barefoot and shirtless if that is your wish and you don't mind catching a cold or the flu. I thought earlier of asking you to share my blanket to keep you warm tonight. However, this dog is choosing to let you sleep in the lodge of the grandmother with no one to put your cold bare feet on to warm."

"I am sorry I have hurt you with my words. They were not intentional. I appreciate all you have done for me today. I am the dog, not you."

"You are not a dog, Gray Feather. You have never been fat, ugly, and unwanted in your life. Words are just words and you are full of them. I am halfway sorry I rescued you today. "

"I promise you, Pansy Sky Walker, that I am not an ugly worded man. I just can't seem to get my words right tonight. One day you will see the respect that I have for you. I see the skinny you inside the large you. I like both of you and want both of you to be my friend."

"A friend would never call me a dog. You are like my father, sister, and tribe." She replied as they pulled off the road and into the Weelo camp.

Gray Feather didn't say anything further for the moment. He already had his foot in his mouth that was going to be hard to get back out.

CHAPTER FIVE

MOON DANCE

As Pansy Sky Walker pulled her old green Cadillac in to the Weelo tribe camp, Gray Feather was surprised to see only one Hogan type dwelling and twenty or so silver, bullet shaped travel trailers. Each of the travel trailers was about sixteen feet long. There were no outside structures such as sheds, barns, or traditional T-Pees. There was just a huge circle of travel trailers with the Hogan being the center like the hub of a wheel. There was also eerie silence. You would think that there would be a dog barking or the blare of someone's television or radio being heard in such a small circle of dwellings, but everything was eerily quiet.

Pansy pulled up in front of the Hogan's door. The only light came from a campfire in front of the Hogan.

"Why aren't there any lights on?" he asked eyeing the quietness and darkness of the camp.

"We are beyond the reaches of electricity and phone lines. We are in the wastelands. We use our backup or battery lighted systems only for emergencies. We get up with the sun and go to bed when it sets."

"You don't watch late night talk shows and news programs?"

"This is a different world here, Gray Feather. You may have had those luxuries in the north. We do not. We get up with the rising of the sun and settle down with its going down. While the mothers are putting the children down to sleep, we move around and sit outside and visit by the light of small campfires. When it goes out, we go to bed. We do not embrace all the materialism and culture of the white man. We live a simple life embracing our tribe's values.

"Which trailer is yours?" he asked as she turned off the car in front of the Hogan structure

"You are sitting in it. I am a half breed, Gray Feather. I am not trusted with one of the tribes silver bullets. You have to be full blooded to be entrusted with one of them. I sleep in this car and keep what possessions I have in the trunk and glove compartment. Before that, I slept in a horse trailer with a tarp thrown over the top.

"Who occupies the Hogan?"

"The grandmother had it built about thirty years ago because she and Grandfather Night Shadow needed room to treat the illnesses of our people and have a place to store things that will not fit into the travel trailers. The Hogan is a storehouse for cases of food bought by the tribe. The grandparents control everything that comes in and is distributed out. Every family, or tribe member, receives exactly the same. We have twenty families in twenty bullets. If ten pairs of shoes come in, one shoe would be given each family. Then it is up to the families to barter amongst themselves to get a matching pair of shoes if they need them. Grandfather Night Shadow always trades his items like that for packs of cigarettes, his addiction. Those that don't smoke are more than glad to trade him their share of cigarettes for his shoe or whatever he has that they need. Whatever you need, you will have to barter and trade for. Your commodity to get started will be your connection to the Great Spirit and the telling of the tribe what you see. They will be required to drop one of their items in your basket that you will keep next to you. In return, you must trade the items in your basket for clothing, shoes, or whatever you feel you have need of. We have four members of our tribe who are truck drivers. They make the bulk of the money that supports the tribe. They take their wages and buy cases of food or whatever the grandparents say the tribe needs. In return, the drivers are allowed so much money to keep as well as first choice of who is available to marry. They also occupy the four seats next to the grandparents at tribal fires which are the same as being princes and princesses in the white man's world. Next to them sits me, the story teller. It is the only honor I have in the tribe. I stretch the truth a lot in my story telling to keep my position. You will be my new story. Three toes and Running Deer are both truckers and single. No one in the tribe can marry until they make a choice or turn down a choice. I cannot marry till three toes states that he doesn't want me. You cannot get married in our tribe unless Running Deer turns you down and says she is not interested in you. The providers always get first choice. They have earned the privilege by feeding and providing for the tribe. Three toes will not choose me because I am a half breed. Pure Weelo is held in esteem in the camp. He is pure Weelo as well as Running Deer."

"So, tonight is not a tribal fire night?"

"No, it is Christmas Eve in the white man's world. In ours it is just another night except for the ones that are currently converted to a white man's religion for one reason or another. Christmas is a good time for us if we are converts. The churches give us shoes and baskets of food which we all share. We accept gifts, but we do not beg or fill out forms for charity."

"Where will I sleep tonight Pansy, my headache is coming back and I don't feel so well." He replied once more starting to hold his head.

"I must introduce you to the tribe leader and then we will lean that seat back and you will sleep like me in this car. I found you in the wasteland of the white men's streets, so you belong to me. If we find something in the desert, it belongs to the one who found it, even if we have lost it and it is quite valuable. The rule teaches the tribe to be careful with their possessions. You are a found possession. I should have kept your white robe and traded it. Someone in the tribe could have cut it up and made baby diapers or bath towels out of it. I wasn't thinking."

Pansy opened her door and got out. An old woman exited the Hogan and greeted her eyeing the stranger in the passenger seat.

"Who is with you, Pansy Sky Walker?" the weathered seventyish woman asked standing in the dark.

"Gray Feather, a medicine man from the north, has made his way to us. I found him in the desert in a brain fog. He was lost."

"Welcome Gray Feather, you are welcome in my lodge."Grandmother Moon Dance stated.

"Gray Feather will stay with me, Grandmother. I found him in the dessert. He is mine." Pansy replied.

"Well, let me take a look at what you found in the desert. He is not answering us. Afterward we will discuss your find. Have you forgotten that Three Toes has the right to choose and you are on his list? You are not free to take a man."

"I am a half-breed, Grandmother Moon Dance. He will not choose me. I am sure he prefers my mother Running Deer. She is his age as well as drives a truck like him. They are right for each other."

"Let me take a look at this medicine man you found in the desert in a brain fog." She said walking over to the passenger side of the fifty some year old rusted green Cadillac that had seen its better days thinking the new medicine man was probably drunk.

"Don't forget, this lost drunk is mine." Pansy Sky Walker once more interjected.

Jo Hammers

"Are you drunk or asleep, Gray Feather?" Grandmother Moon Dance inquired.

Gray Feather just looked at her, but didn't answer.

"He is definitely drunk, grandmother. However, he has a powerful connection with the Great Spirit, but not much of a sense of direction." Pansy stated speaking for Gray Feather. "He was over three hundred miles away from here and lost in a brain fog. I think he may have encountered the door knockers and they drove him crazy with their words and literature. I found him in the middle of a Texas desert road near one of their great halls. Since I found him in the dessert lands of the white man, I am claiming him as my possession and proclaim my right to him as a man."

"Why is he holding his head and why doesn't he answer, Pansy Sky Walker?"

"He has had a headache off and on all day. The door knocker s probably gave it to him. If not them, I think my father possibly gave him moonshine to drink and he has a bad hangover."

Grandmother Moon Dance leaned into the car and eyed Gray Feather who was sitting holding his head. She could see in the moonlight that he was in pain. She could also see that he was the handsomest Indian man she had ever laid her eyes on.

"The Great Spirit has definitely smiled on him." The leathered old medicine woman replied. "Is he single? Did you leave a wife in the dessert belonging to him?"

"I found him and he was alone, grandmother. His mind is in a fog. He cannot remember anything before yesterday morning. However, keep in mind that he is mine. I found him. I don't care if he is crazy and has no mind."

"We must get him out of the car and into the Hogan. I just don't understand why our men think they have to drink to prove themselves to be men. It looks like we have another drunk to add to our tribal collection."

Gray Feather was ignoring the two women. He felt like his head was swelling and he once more was sick as a dog feeling like he might throw up.

The two women opened the car door, half pulled him from the car, put their arms under his and half carried him into the Hogan and lay him on a rug beneath the kitchen window. His legs were rubbery and he quit answering the two women. Reclined on the rug on the ground beneath the kitchen window of the Hogan, he slipped into the land of nowhere. Instantly, Grandmother Moon Dance knew something was wrong. His eyes in the dark looked like they were rolled back in his head and he had a huge swollen lump on one side of his head.

"You are a half breed idiot, Pansy Sky Walker! Why have you brought a seriously injured man to our camp? We don't have the facilities available to care for him. It looks like he may have broken his crystal skull. That can only be repaired on the Great Mother Ship. Crystal repair is beyond the technology we have here and the Great Mother may not be here for another ten years. Why in the hell did you let your father in Texas give him moonshine to drink? Are you crazy? Haven't you seen what alcohol and drugs of the white man have done to Night Shadow and some of the other men?"

"I did not do this to him. I found him in this condition and assumed he was in a drunk's hangover fog."

"Your mother should have thrown you to the wolves when you were born. You have no Weelo common sense, Pansy Sky Walker. You should have taken him to the nearest hospital. I am not sure that I can save him. He is slipping into the land of spirits from which most ill men don't return. Get out of this Hogan so I can do my thing. Find Leaping Lizard and send her to me. She will need to take the grandfather to stay in her sky flyer till I tend to this medicine man. He may have a virus or something that the grandfather might catch and die from. He is old and feeble. I am old. This could be a disaster that could possibly kill us off as a race. The small pox just about got us in the days of the pioneers. It is forbidden in the tribe to bring anyone with an illness into our midst, or have you forgotten?"

"I didn't know he was ill." Pansy shot back in defense.

"Your white side rules you and your thinking. You will be left behind when the great Mother ship comes. The Great Mother ship is for the intellectual scientists of our planet. You are far from being a Weelo with a great brain. You shame the tribe over and over again with your trips to the land of Texas and a father who has made it clear to you that he does not want you."

"Someday you will pay for those words, Moon Dance. I am not afraid of you like the others." Pansy shouted and left the old woman to tend to Gray Feather. Looking back over her shoulder she shouted," I am not an imbecile!"

Pansy shuffled her three hundred pounds off into the shadows of the camp.

After Pansy left, Grandmother Moon Dance retrieved a flashlight from beside her sleeping rug and returned to the side of Gray Feather and turned it on. That is when she saw that his eyes were rolled back in his head. She immediately got a pan of water and went to washing his face and body trying to revive him. She pulled his tight jeans off and in spite of being stressed, snickered when she saw he had on boxer shorts with animals all over them. Then she quickly removed them and bathed him for twenty minutes to cool him down. She could tell from his hot flesh and perspiration that he was running a serious human fever and the desert air was not helping it. He had slipped into a coma and only the Great Spirit and her nursing skills could save him.

There was no taking him to a hospital or calling 911. When you were Weelo and become ill in the wasteland, you lived or died. If he died they would bury him and send word to the northern tribe that he had died. Three Toes would carry the message when he went out on a long haul that direction in his semi. The Weelo tribe did not fill out birth or death reports with the US government. They kept to themselves and waited for the Great Mother Ship to return for them.

Grandmother Moon Dance continually bathed his naked body thru the night to keep him cool and cared for him by the beams of her flashlight. He was at the point of death and she knew it. She had sat at the bed of her sons and watched them die. She couldn't let this medicine man die like the nurses did her sons in the white man's hospital after their car wreck. The Great Spirit had sent her this man and she needed him.

Seventy year old Grandmother Moon Dance cared for the medicine man in his late twenties and couldn't help but admire how magnificent he was. She was an old woman, but he made her heart race. He was one of the handsomest Indian men she had ever laid her eyes on. Pansy said he was Weelo, but she had her doubts. He had chest hair as well as hair on his legs and face. He had what the white man called a four o'clock shadow. He did have the long black Indian hair, but she was not sure he was Indian. Indian men, as a rule, didn't have facial or body hair. As she looked at how beautiful he was, she wished she was young again. This man was the most magnificent male creature ever and he made her feel like a woman again. The Grandfather had ignored her for years. She was extremely lonely. Rejection as a woman is not an easy thing to live with. Grandfather Night Shadow, her husband, had lost interest in her years before when she was grieving over the death of her four sons who had died a in a car wreck. Wild Cat, her youngest and only living son, was now grown and a truck driver that she saw briefly every two or three weeks. Her husband ignored her other than when it was time to eat or get his hair braided.

"She cried a tear for herself as she cared for this very ill good looking young man about the age of her youngest son. He sparked the woman in her that she thought was dead. However, she could never let anyone know that. She was a respected medicine woman, not an old fool. She had watched old men of the tribe chase young girls and think with their yanker instead of their brain. She was an old woman and he was way too young for her. She would not be an old fool. Gray

46

Feather was probably twenty- seven or twenty eight in her opinion. She was seventy. She would just have to be a secret admirer and she definitely admired what she was seeing. If she were younger in human years, he could put his moccasins under her bed anytime. Then she reminded herself that she was married.

For two weeks, Gray Feather slipped in and out of consciousness. Grandmother Moon Dance didn't leave his side and cared for his every need. When he was conscious, he clung to her crying. She held him like a baby and fed him herbal teas. When he took the cold chills, she crawled beneath his blanket to him to warm him. When his fever raged she bathed him to keep him cool.

On the fifteenth day, he opened his eyes about ten in the morning and looked into the smiling, weathered face of the grandmother. She had gentle brown eyes that seemed like they could see straight thru him. Over her shoulders fell two gray braids. Half of her teeth were missing making her look haggard and tired.

"You have the Great Spirit's eyes," he whispered trying to sit up. "I have been to the other side and there saw a great big ship. I was told it was the Great Mother Ship. There was a man there with crystal ears who said he was the Great Spirit. He told my soul to return to you and tell you that he will come for you in about six to seven years. I wanted to stay in the sky with him where I had no headache. He sent me back to you saying that I was to tie our braids together someday. I do not know what he meant by it."

"You are a great medicine man, Gray Feather. Only the chosen are granted permission for an audience with the Great Spirit. You are a soul flyer. I know what the six to seven years means. I have cared for you and the Great Spirit has in turn sent me some much needed information. You will not leave my house, Gray Feather. You are a stronger medicine man than me or the Grandfather. Neither of us have seen or been granted an audience with the Great Spirit since we have resided in human bodies."

"The man with the crystal ears told me to obey you because you own me. I will obey you, Grandmother Moon Dance because I love you, not because you own me. I know I would be dead if it hadn't been for your arms loving and caring for me."

"The Great Spirit has given me a great treasure," she stated helping him to sit up. Then she took got a comb and prepared to braid his hair for the day. You will remain in my lodge. I will continue to care for you. You are a soul flyer, Gray Feather. Our other soul flyer died many generations ago on top of a mountain in a flood. He was medicine man when the Great Mother Ship crashed and all of the animals were loosed upon the Earth."

"This soul flyer owes you my life. I have felt your body next to me warming me and your hands and a wet rag cooling me. When I regain my strength, you will be my number one girl. I am sorry you have had to look at my nakedness and clean up my filth. You are a stranger, yet you have taken me in and cared for me." He whispered as she helped him to sit up and sip from a cup of tea.

The Grandmother grinned and steadied him. She could never tell anyone that she had enjoyed looking at him as well as lying next to him to warm him. She had done everything in her power to save him, but she was also Weelo guilty of peeping at the body of the handsomest man that she had ever seen. The Indian men of her tribe were dogs next to him.

Back in Bullhorn, Texas, Ralph Archer was packing his friend's suitcase to check out of the hotel where they had been staying. Michael, his best man, just disappeared off the face of the planet. A missing person's report had been filed. Doctor Archer was just short of a mental breakdown not knowing what had happened to his lifelong best friend. As he was stuffing things in his friend's shaving kit, he spotted a little red jewelry box. He opened it and grinned seeing that an engagement ring was inside. Apparently, Michael had bought the ring in Ft. Worth when they stayed all night there on their way to Bullhorn. His friend was dating a nurse back in New Jersey named Jennifer. He was pleased seeing the ring. Apparently Michael intended to propose to her when they returned home. They had always done everything together apparently getting engaged and married together in the same year.

He hurried and finished their packing. He had to return to New Jersey to escape Pete Carlson and his men who were stalking him for having dumped his bride at the altar. The FBI had informed him they would keep in touch with any news. Doctor Ralph Archer just couldn't accept that his friend could possibly be dead and the victim of foul play. However, there was no trace of him and it had been somewhere around a month since they ran from the church on Christmas Eve dumping his bride. He was sure that Connie's father and his rifle toting hired help may possibly have killed Michael by mistake thinking he was him.

Over a month passed before Gray Feather was able to regain his strength and venture outside of the Hogan. The grandmother placed him a small hand woven rug just outside the Hogan door. After breakfast each morning, he sat and spoke with whoever came along. All the tribe respected the fact that he had been very ill and they shared with him anything in their store that they felt might help him to regain his health. They paid for their sitting talks with a piece of fruit or healing teas to brew. All were surprised to find out that he didn't eat meat or wear items from leather. They were also pleased that Gray Feather always shared whatever was in his basket with the Great Grandmother. If it was a candy bar, he split it with her. They saw him as an honorable man. Gray Feather became a member of the grandparent's house and slept beneath the kitchen window on a rug on the ground.

Gray Feather did not regain his memory but accepted the fact that Pansy had told him that he was a Weelo medicine man.

To Pansy's dismay, Grandmother Moon Dance refused to let Pansy claim Gray Feather as her property having found him in the desert. She never mentioned that she had actually taken him from a side street in Bullhorn, Texas. That would not be in the desert in the Tribe's eyes. Grandmother Moon Dance stated that Three Toes hadn't turned Pansy down as a wife yet. She claimed Gray Feather on the grounds that she had earned the right to him because she had saved his life. Pansy was yelling mad, but the tribe stood behind Grandmother Moon Dance because they knew she had nursed him for thirty days and that Pansy was promised to Three Toes till he turned her down.

Doctor Michael Haven, who was now known as Gray Feather, didn't recall his life as a veterinarian or a popular New Jersey bachelor. He accepted the fact that he had been on a bad drunk and his mind had slipped into a fog. He didn't question his life sleeping on a rug by the kitchen window of the grandparent's Hogan. He didn't question anything. He slept on his rug, helped the grandmother with the housework, and sat on his hand braided rug outside the lodge door and counseled whoever came along. Grandfather Night Shadow, who was at least eighty, was showing early signs of dementia. Some days he joined in on the conversations, other days he ignored them wandering off or just napping on his rug. He ignored Gray Feather most of the time. Grandmother Moon Dance and Gray Feather bonded and attended all functions of the tribe together. Pansy Sky Walker seethed.

The evenings with the tribe was what Gray Feather enjoyed the most. When the sun would start to set, the tribe would come out of their travel trailers to socialize. The men built small bonfires from skids left on the provider's trucks. Everyone sat around sharing stories, smoking cigarettes, and drinking whatever was available. Pansy Sky Walker was the story teller for the people and was the nightly entertainment. She told tales of great ships with animals on them. She told tales of their tribe flying silver bullets over a land called the Dakotas and being chased by US fighter jets. The children loved that story. She also told a tale about Gray Feather and the Goose Spirit that moved across the dessert like a side winder rattlesnake claiming its wings. Pansy told stories of the birth of medicine men, chiefs, and women warriors. She told of hunting trips, marriages, and the births of twins which were revered in the tribe. She was a story teller, an oral history book of the tribe.

Michael Haven, now Gray Feather, was sure that Pansy could be a great writer. She had the knack of putting her own spin on her stories, stretching them and making them interesting. He was also sure that Pansy was a Sci-Fi buff. That was okay with him. He liked women that were different and had a brief flash of a memory of knowing a woman who ate raw fish and danced in a wire cage. However, he couldn't remember who she was or where he knew her from. He remembered flashing lights all around her and men's voices laughing all around him. The men went to town occasionally on drinking binges. He was sure that he must have seen her in a bar on one of those trips. He did lose his memory due to a drunken binge that he deeply regretted.

Late in the evening, Gray Feather would walk over to the old rusted green convertible where Pansy slept and chat leaning against her car. They were fairly close to the same age and he felt comfortable talking to her. Grandmother Moon Dance had explained to him that Three Toes and Pansy were promised. So, he never opened the passenger side car door and got in. Tribal marriages and promises were taken seriously.

Pansy weighed over three hundred pounds and Gray Feather was concerned that her obesity was going to kill her. He spoke to her about weight loss, but nothing seemed to get thru to her. When she came home from visits to the land of Texas, she brought home bags and bags of cookies and doughnuts. Gray Feather was sure that she would be dead in a year or so if she didn't change her eating habits. He also knew that there was a woman inside of Pansy's huge body that he had feelings for. He had felt his heart racing for her the moment she had rescued him from the center of the street when he entered his brain fog. He loved her stories and knew that she needed to embrace the lifestyle of the white man and become a writer. He seemed to remember that he once loved books. He just couldn't put a face on the man inside him who loved books.

Gray Feather had feelings for Pansy but he was also struggling with the idea that he might have a wife and children in the north that he had forgotten. He could tell by looking at his body that he had to be nearing thirty. Most thirty year old men were married and had children. Somehow, he knew he was Catholic and he believed in being committed to one woman for life. The name Carol Sue bugged him. It was possible that he was married to a white woman. Carol Sue was not an Indian name.

Gray Feather was lonely for arms to hold him. He wanted the warmth of a woman's body next to him. His rug beneath the kitchen window of Grandmother Moon Dance was lonely and a cold bed to sleep in.

CHAPTER SIX

BACK IN NEW JERSEY

Doctor Ralph Archer collapsed after returning to New Jersey without his lifelong friend, Michael Haven. He couldn't function knowing that he had possibly been the cause of the death of his friend due to his asking him to be the best man at his wedding. He voluntarily entered the psychiatric ward of St. Francis Hospital and escaped his stress diving head first into the world of tranquilizers and liquor.

A nationwide search was being conducted with the town of Bullhorn, Texas as the hub of the wheel. Law enforcement was convinced that the doctor was buried somewhere on the Carlson's ranch or had been ground into dog food in the Carlson's processing plant. The irony was that whoever had abducted the fleeing angel groom had gotten the wrong man. Both the groom and the best man had been wearing identical white robes and wings. It was the best man missing, not the groom.

When not high on drugs, Ralph replayed the pre-wedding fiasco over and over in his mind trying to make sense of what might have happened to his friend. He beat himself up mentally for the fact that the two of them didn't stick together after the wedding instead of running in two different directions. He remembered Pete Carlson yelling, "Get Him." Also, he recalled the sounds of people following him out the church door and down the steps. He remembered Michael telling him to run and not look back. He couldn't come up with any concrete ideas as to which direction Michael ran or who was chasing him mistaking him for the groom. However, guns were drawn at the wedding and he remembered gun shots. He was sure Pete Carlson had murdered and dumped his friend somewhere on his ranch in the Texas dessert, although he couldn't prove it.

Taking a sip of water from a water bottle on the stand next to his hospital bed, Ralph replayed the voices at the wedding trying to remember anything that was said that might be a clue. He then beat himself up for not sticking with Michael.

He had gotten his friend killed and that he couldn't handle. The idea that Michael could be laying dead and rotting in the desert somewhere had pushed him to the brink of suicide.

He recalled waiting at the motel for hours and then going and looking for Michael finding the streets around the church empty and the Carlson wedding party gone. He recalled wandering into the police station about midnight and declaring Michael missing. Then he recalled endless days of waiting for news and then a flight home without his friend.

A phone call interrupted his thoughts as he sat in his hospital bed high on psychiatric stress relievers.

"Dr. Archer speaking," He answered.

"Don't hang up, Ralph! I need your help. The FBI is considering arresting my father for the murder of your friend. I need you to call them and tell them he didn't do it." Connie Carlson shouted in a stressed voice.

"I don't know that you or your father didn't kill Michael. There were gunshots and I was running like crazy to get a way." He retorted stressed that she had the nerve to call him.

"It was an old car backfiring, Ralph. It happened just after dad and I exited the church behind you. We yelled and threatened Michael thinking he was you, but we did not shoot him. We agree something has happened to your friend, but it wasn't at our hands. Please call and talk to the FBI telling them about the old car backfiring. Our reputation here is ruined here thanks to you and your friend. We are considered possible murderers. Daddy's boys might have roughed you up a little if they had caught up with you, but they wouldn't have killed you."

"That is nice to know, Connie. Your damn redneck father and his boys have without a doubt killed Michael thinking he was me. When the FBI finds Michael's body, you and your asshole father are going to pay."

"You think I haven't paid a price? You dumped me at the altar in front of all my family and friends?" She shouted back. "You have ruined my life. Everyone here is laughing at me."

"Michael and I have been friends since grade school. We are like brothers. You have stolen from me a part of my life that I don't think I can live without. He is my family."

"Eye for an eye . . . Is that what you want Ralph? You lose your friend so you take my dad? I am the victim, not you or your friend. You led me on, slept with me, promised to marry me and then dumped me at the altar. It doesn't get more degrading than that. Your friend is out there and possibly dead, but not at the hands of me and my father. When this is over, you owe me a big apology for using me, dumping me, and letting me and my father pay for your decision to fly away like angels. Both of you deserve to die in my book. Maybe some day after he is found, I will have the opportunity to shoot your ass."

"I made a bad decision asking you to marry me and it has cost me my best friend. Don't call me, Connie! I have enough to deal with without you trying to get me to lie for your father."

"Don't hang up, Ralph!" She quickly stated and hurriedly added, "My father asked me to offer you a hundred grand if you will go to the feds and say you have heard from Michael."

"You have got to be kidding. You think I would sell my friend out for a hundred thousand dollars?" he yelled over the phone in disgust.

"I personally think my father should shoot your ass and let you join your friend in whatever ditch someone has put him in. However, at the moment, we are at your mercy. We are not guilty of killing your friend. However, I will admit that I have considered killing your ass myself a few times over the last few weeks. You embarrassed the hell out of me in front of my sister and friends dumping me at the altar. My father has always preferred my sister to me. She was there gloating and saw the whole thing. How could you do that to me?" She yelled mad.

"Throw me in a ditch along with my friend? " Raphael Archer asked in shock and then slammed the phone down hanging up on the woman he had come so close to marrying. His friend had saved him from her and paid the price for it. He rang for the nurse.

"Yes, Doctor Archer?"

"I think you had better call and get me a sleeping pill from my doctor and put me on suicide watch. If I don't kill myself having a stroke from my stress, my ex-fiancé is going to do it. She just called offering me a hundred thousand dollars to lie and say Michael has called me. I need you to call the FBI for me and give them that information. The number is in my billfold that you have locked up in your hospital office safe. "

The nurse replied in a serious voice, "I was listening at your door, Ralph. I heard you yelling and was headed into your room to check on you when I heard the conversation between you and Connie. She was yelling so loud on the phone that I could hear her to. I will retrieve your billfold from the office and help you with your phone call." She stated and then added. "I feel just as guilty as you do Ralph. I have told myself over and over that Michael might be here with us had I accompanied him to Texas. Maybe the whole chain of events would have been different."

"Things are what they are, Jennifer. I am guilty and you feel guilty when it is the person who has done something to him that is the guilty one. I keep trying to tell myself that I am not responsible, but I am. Had I asked Jack Benson to be my best man, Michael would be mad about it but he would be alive and with us. You know that the FBI feels he is dead because it has been weeks and there has been no activity on any of his credit cards or bank accounts."

"It is a hard thing to accept, Ralph. Eventually, you and I are going to have to accept the fact, grieve, and move on. The one thing that Michael would not abandon under any circumstances is his dog Carol Sue. She was the last gift given him by his parents before they died."

"I know you are right, I just don't want to accept it. The Kennel says they have had no contact from Michael. I picked Carol Sue up last week. My housekeeper is watching her till I come to grips with my stress. I have honestly thought about taking my life, Jennifer. Michael is like a brother to me and the only family I have. You know that I am an orphan. Losing him is like losing part of me."

"You said the big word suicide, Ralph. Now, I am going to have to put you on suicide watch? You are going to be sleeping on the floor in a padded cell without furniture or phone cord to strangle yourself on." Jennifer stated thinking of the times her and Michael had spent together. They were both vegetarians as well as animal rights activists. They weren't in love, although they slept together. They were comfortable with each other and respected each other's eating habits and quirks. A vegetarian male your age was hard to come by. Michael hated dating women that expected to be taken to steak houses on dates and she was the same. She couldn't find a man who was willing to throw away his steak knife. Her and Michael were comfortable with each other and enjoyed eating out together and doing charity work concerning animal rights. They were compatible.

"Well, a padded room can't be any worse that the pens I put my four footed patients in after surgery. Bring it on. Could you at least throw in a bag of cookies for my midnight snack? I am used to treating all of the animals out at the vet hospital to doggie biscuits and tuna chews at midnight when I check on them. I am used to having a cookie with them. Don't tell anyone, but I sit down in the floor so they can see me eating like them. I like the one on one eye contact with them. There are times when I think I can read their minds."

"I think a bag of animal cookies can be arranged." She laughed.

He laughed back in response to her laughter. She had a beautiful voice. "If you want some night, you can come out to the clinic and sit with me in the floor analyzing my animal's mental state. I don't know about them, but I could use a good psychiatric nurse to make me fetch, heel, and roll over. I might even enjoy a little tummy scratch or two."

"Will I find fleas should I scratch your tummy?" She replied humorously.

"Shared fleas can really drive a woman and man crazy. I would be willing to itch a little with you."

"Maybe someday, Ralph. For now, I am too guilty to consider dating anyone but Michael. I just always assumed that one day the two of us would tie the knot. We were comfortable with each other and enjoyed doing things together."

"I always assumed that Michael would be my friend for a lifetime. Choosing and making a new friend is not going to be easy. We had the same interests and could read each other like books."

"In case I haven't told you, I thought you looked real cute in that cross dresser, winged angel costume that hit the national news. Why didn't you wear a white tux which is more appropriate for a male angel?"

"Why do you think I am in here in the nut ward? My office staff is snickering behind my back. My barber asked me if I was going to bring the goose in for wing grooming. My banker asked me if I had changed careers and took up acting. His daughter was getting married and he wanted me to stand as an angel behind the minister and flap my wings and sing Bless This House. My respectable life is in the toilet and with it I have lost my best friend." I need to be kenneled for awhile where I am safe. I know I have some serious mental issues, Jennifer. I am a doctor."

"Give me five minutes and I will be in with a sleeper pill, your billfold, and a bag of cookies. We keep animal crackers on the floor for kids who end up her occasionally. I think you might be the biggest juvenile that we have had recently."

"Make it three bags of the animal crackers and I will make your next doggie visit to my clinic free."

"It's a deal, Doc." She answered and the communication went dead.

"On the fourth day of his self imposed commitment to the psychiatric ward, Ralph's cell phone rang. He answered thinking that it was possibly his housekeeper with a complaint about Carol Sue of some sort.

"Doctor Archer speaking. . ." He answered.

"Doctor Archer, this is agent Shelley with the FBI. I have called to tell you that we have found Dr. Haven's jeans, billfold, shirt, and tennis shoes as well as your tennis shoes and shirt. Your jeans were not amongst the items found."

"Is he alive?" Ralph asked hating to have to ask it.

"Dr. Haven was not with the items of clothing we have found. A rental truck company had your friend's items in their lost and found. A man renting a truck to move in found the items in the back. Do you have any idea how your friends clothing and billfold might have ended up in Oregon?"

"Oregon . . . you found Michael's billfold and clothes in Oregon?" Ralph asked in shock.

"Yes, they were found in the back of a rental moving truck in Oregon and the company tossed them in their lost and found box till they could get around to tracing down the owner of the billfold."

"We have gone on vacations our whole lives together, but never to Oregon. We are the Colorado ski lodge types or Florida beach bums. As far as I know neither of us has ever been to Oregon."

"A man from Oregon turned in the found items to the rental truck agency thinking the person before him had lost them. When the supervisor of the rental truck place saw a rerun of the flying angels on the national news he recognized the names and compared Dr. Haven's name to the billfold in their lost and found discovering they had clues to his disappearance. The man who rented the truck and turned the billfold in is long gone. He signed on to an Alaskan fishing vessel after storing whatever was in the truck. We got a warrant and looked thru his storage locker. There was no sign of your friend there."

"What are you trying to tell me?" Ralph asked.

"There are two possibilities. One your friend has met foul play somewhere between Texas and Oregon, or your friend has dumped his identity as Dr. Michael Haven and has signed on as a cook on a fishing boat. Is the second scenario possible?"

"No, the second is not possible. Michael is a poor swimmer and terrified of water. He was in a boating accident when he was five. He watched his grandparents and a small sister drown. He won't vacation anywhere that he has to fly over water. When we are on the beach in Florida, he never steps a foot into the water because of his fear. My friend is a panty waist when it comes to water. He had the bathtubs removed from his new house and showers only installed."

"Considering that he hasn't used his credit cards or made any withdrawals from his checking account since the dump the bride event occurred, you must resign yourself to the fact that your friend has to be dead and most likely from foul play."

"You aren't going to quit looking for him, are you?" Doctor Archer gulped fighting back tears. His folly with Connie Carlson had possibly caused the death of his best friend. He didn't know how he was going to live with himself.

"We have an agent now flying out to the fishing boat to see if the cook is Dr. Haven. If he isn't, then we are going to question him how the items came into his possession. We do know that he loaded his truck in Bullhorn, Texas a block east of the church and a couple blocks down on a side street. Being Christmas Eve, there weren't a lot of residents home. People were out doing last minute Christmas shopping etc. We couldn't find anyone who was at home during the time the rental truck was parked in the area near the church."

"Michael had to be seen by someone!"

"Forty-eight hours are long past, Dr. Archer. It has been a month or more. We are presuming that your friend is most likely dead. The cook on the fishing boat may surprise us and turn out to be him. Personally, I have my doubts after hearing your story about Dr. Haven's phobia of water."

Raphael Archer hung up the phone and broke into tears. How could he have been so stupid and let this tragedy happen. Then a light bulb in his head went on and he remembered what Connie had said about an old car that was backfiring in front of the church that everyone assumed was gun fire. Was it possible that the driver of the old car could have picked up his friend offering him a ride to escape Connie and Pete Carlson? Was the driver of the old car some lowlife sociopath criminal? As soon as he was out of the hospital, he was going to hire a private detective in Texas to find out. He would ask the detective to check all of the photos that the people were snapping of the fleeing angels to see if there was an old car in the back ground of any of them. There were four hundred guests at the wedding. Surely one of them would remember the old car or took a photo with it in it. He couldn't give up looking for Michael as long as there was any clue at all. If Michael was dead, he owed him a proper funeral and a lifetime of grief.

CHAPTER SEVEN

A NEW OCCUPATION

Two months had passed and Gray Feather had gained his strength back. However, he still had an occasional headache. His memory, however, was lost in his fog somewhere with only an occasional premonition that he knew this or that. The Weelo tribe had accepted him as their new medicine man. He accepted what Pansy told him. He was a medicine man from the north tribe who drank white lightening causing his memory to take flight. She said she had been sent to find him on the day he arrived and she had followed him drunk from a bar and saved him from getting run over in a drunken state. He had no memories, so he relied on what she told him and tried to fit in with the tribe and the elderly grandmother who had nursed him back to health.

The medicine woman, Grandmother Moon Dance, took him in. He willfully became her right hand in everything. The grandfather was old and only interested in smoking and wandering off with the men to play cards or drink out of sight of the camp. Gray Feather stayed close to Grandmother Moon Dance seeing himself as belonging to her. He respected her and did whatever she said like he was some young kid. She was his anchor, his stability. When you have no memories, you cling to the person you are making new memories with. Grandmother Moon Dance was his new world and he stayed close to her in case his headaches returned or should he become deathly ill again. He feared being away from her.

Grandmother Moon Dance let Gray Feather sit next to her outside the Hogan for a couple of months observing her counseling the tribe members. At the end of two months when he was feeling well again, she provided him with two little hand loomed sitting rugs.

"These are yours to sit outside the lodge on. One is for you and the other for the tribal member which wishes to inquire advice from you. This basket is for your inquirers to place their payment for your services in. You do not need to set a price for your services. It will be up to the tribal member to decide and he will put in your basket what he deems appropriate. Tomorrow, you will start your new work here as a medicine man. You are a man; you will sit by the front door. I will sit at the rear of the Hogan and spread my two rugs there. We will both be practicing our craft, but we will have two separate exam rooms like the white man doctors have. Mine will be in the rear and you in the front of the Hogan."

"Thank you, Grandmother Moon Dance. May I ask why you are letting me counsel the tribe's members?" I still have no memories. My brain fog has not gone away."

"Today you will start reading the sky for the members of our tribe. If you don't have an answer, look to the sky and tell them what shapes you see in the clouds. We all are looking for personal signs. We will interpret what you see and your brain will not have to worry itself with interpreting.'

"What if there are no clouds?" he asked.

"Then eye the desert Ravens and tell the tribe what you see them doing that reminds you of people."

"What if there are no Ravens?" he asked.

"If you are that desperate, rise and run around the Hogan to where I sit. I will give you a quick word and you can run back around the Hogan and tell your rug sitter that you had to run and inquire of a greater spirit than you. "She laughed and then continued. "Speaking to a spirit greater than you during counseling time will cost you one item from your payment basket."

"I see, I am a professional medicine man, but you are a specialist." He replied grinning. He had learned to love the seventy year old woman dearly. There was something about her eyes that seemed to look thru him and see what he needed and she was always there for him. He wished he had some way of repaying her for all the kindness.

"I guess you could look at it that way, Gray Feather. Run around the Hogan if you need me." She replied with her toothy grin.

Gray Feather wished he had met her years ago. He would have seen to it that she had dental care. He wondered if he had a living mother and dad somewhere. Somehow he didn't feel that he did. It was just a feeling. He didn't know it for sure. What he did know was that he loved Grandmother Moon Dance and no one was going t o mess with her because she was the only family he had. He liked Grandfather Night Shadow, but the bonding wasn't there like it was between him and the grandmother. He secretly thought the grandfather treated her callously looking at younger women when she was not watching. Gray Feather was thankful to have a roof over his head, so he kept his mouth shut. He didn't want to be sleeping in the back of a horse trailer with a tarp thrown over it.

"Will you sit with me and let me practice once on you? He asked pointing to the spot where he had spread his rugs.

"I will sit just as long as you do not read my mind. There is a secret there that I do not want anyone to know." She replied sitting slowly down on the ground on the inquirer's rug.

Gray Feather sat down next to her and crossed his legs like she had done. "What would you ask of the Great Spirit this morning, Moon Dance?" he asked dropping the grandmother. She was a woman sitting inquiring not a grandmother.

"I wish to know how many maidens Night Shadow has been eyeing this week. I am thinking of setting his boots outside my door. One wandering eye is acceptable, maybe two. I could put out two eyes and make him quit looking. However, if it is more than he has eyes, then I must hobble both of his legs and feet so that he cannot wander. Night Shadow told me last night that I have lost my appeal as a woman. I fear he is looking for a reason to divorce me. Ask the Great Spirit for insight into my problem."

"Hold that thought," Gray Feather stated rising. He then run around the Hogan and sat down on the other side of the grandmother. Gray Feather could tell by the look on her face and her snicker that she was amused by him. "Doctor Moon Dance, I have a woman on my counseling rug who wants to know how many maidens her husband has been looking at and should she hobble him. I have come to the specialist for an opinion." He stated grinning.

"Go back and tell the woman on your sitting rug that he has been looking at Running Deer and one of the teens named Prickly Pear. Also tell her not to hobble her husband yet. He is old and might die of natural causes soon. Tell her that she would be wasting energy that she might need for a second husband." She replied with a full grin and snickering.

This time Gray Feather broke out in a snort. "You are very wise, Doctor Moon Dance. What do I owe you?"

"Whatever the woman on your rug pays you." She replied trying to contain laughter.

Gray Feather rose and ran back around the Hogan and sat down on his rug that he was to counsel on. Looking over at Moon Dance he grinned and bit his lip to keep from losing his composure. He could see in her sparkling eyes that she was about to burst into laughter. "I have a word for you Moon Dance from a spirit that is greater than I."

"What is it, respected medicine man?" she asked controlling her need to laugh. She loved the fact that he had taken her seriously and had run all the way around the Hogan to inquire of her as a medicine woman.

"Do not worry about the two maidens the grandfather eyes. He is old and will probably die soon and you should save your energy for the second husband that you will take. Also, the Great Spirit above us says that the secret in your heart will one day be yours if you are patient. The Great Spirit says he sees all, knows all, and hears all. He knows that Night Shadow disrespects you. The Great Spirit says seven crows will eat seven sets of twelve moons. When the seventh set of moons is about completed, you will love another and he will love you, the secret of your heart." Gray Feather stated wondering where the words about the crows and moons came from.

Grandmother Moon Dance jumped up as quickly as an old woman could and stared down at him as he sat cross legged. Her face was full of questions and seriousness. "You are a soul flyer and a carrier of messages from the Great Mother Ship. I know what the seven crows and seven sets of moons mean. This is a great moment in time for our people. We have not had a medicine man who hears the signal voice of the Great Spirit and the Mother Ship for many years. Be prepared for a full day of reading from here on out. All of the tribe must inquire of you for guidance before your fog lifts. One day you will leave us. I saw in a night dream that you will only be with us for a short time and afterward the tribe will scatter. Only seven black braids will wait seven years for the seven sets of moons to be completed. They are the chosen to return to the sky. I must go to Hissing Cat and tell her of your prophecy. She is ancient and she must know to hold on for a few more years till regeneration comes."

"You are not going anywhere till you pay me," he stated biting his lip to keep from being amused with her. He had seen seven black ravens behind the Hogan when he had run around it.

"Oh . . . I do owe you payment." she stated and then motioned for him to bend down. She then kissed him on the cheek. "That is your payment, what I feel your counseling is worth."

"Thank you Moon Dance, now stand here till I run around the Hogan and pay the specialist." He stated grinning at her. Then he ran around the Hogan and ended up on the other side of her panting. He still wasn't quite up to par. His concussion and the weeks of lying around recuperating had weakened his body. "I have come to pay you, Doctor Moon Dance for your services." He stated. "What is your charge?

"As I told you before, whatever your sitter placed into your payment basket is what I am to be paid. It better be good, this specialist doesn't work cheap." She stated snickering.

"Well, close your eyes Doctor Moon Dance and I am going to pay you. I don't want you to see how cheap my payment is. You must feel how much it is."

"Are you one of those dead beat tribal members who try to skip out on paying me? Do you plan to run when I close my eyes?" she asked grinning.

"I am an honest tribal member. Now, close your eyes." He stated grinning like a cat that ate a canary. "Don't open them till I have made full payment. Do you understand?"

"I understand, Gray Feather. Now pay up or shut up. I have clients coming and a busy morning planned. I am a specialist you know." She stated with her eyes closed in her aged leathered face.

Twenty eight year old Gray Feather stepped to her and folded his arms around her and picked her up off the ground hugging her tight and let her feet dangle. Then he nuzzled his unshaven face next to her leathered one and listened to her squeal from the scratching of his beard. Then he whispered in her ear as he held her tight, "I can never repay you for all you have done for me. The only thing I have to give you is my words. I love you deeply and always will. Should the grandfather ever divorce you, you will not be alone. You cared for me when I was a stranger in a fog. This stranger owes you his life. As an Indian man, I can choose who I wed. I promise you I will take you as my wife if the grandfather ever disrespects you. I will care for you till the day you pass over to the next life. You are my number one girl and always will be." Then he kissed her on her cheek and let her down.

Grandmother Moon Dance opened her eyes and grinned. "I might hold you to that someday. You should be careful what you pay a medicine woman with. I would be the envy of all the females on the Great Mother ship having a young Indian buck choose to marry me."

"Just so we are clear on the subject, Three Toes cannot ask for you because I have already made my claim and I am higher ranking than him." He replied holding his head high, crossing his arms across his chest in Indian fashion, and then winking at her. Then he turned and ran back around the building and stood facing her. She hadn't sat back down. "Do you have anything further to ask of the Great Spirit?" he asked her in a serious voice.

"Just thank the Great Spirit for me for the wonderful young brave he has sent my way to watch out for me in my old age. I am pleased with his gift." She said and walked away whistling.

CHAPTER EIGHT

COUNSELING THE TRIBE

The first six months seemed to fly by. In the mornings, Gray Feather helped Grandmother Moon Dance cook breakfast and then cleanup. After breakfast till mid afternoon, he counseled whoever showed up to sit on the rug next to him. Most of his sitters were women with questions about everything from child birth to why their biscuits wouldn't rise. The children were always the most fun asking how to catch a rabbit or how to make their siblings disappear. Gray Feather loved his new life, but wondered often what his old one was like.

For the last week or so, Gray Feather had been deeply concerned concerning Pansy Sky Walker. He knew that she was putting on more weight and was approaching four hundred pounds. After the evening meal and clean up, Gray Feather was free to roam about the camp and talk to the tribe members as they sat outside their campers around small family bonfires. He played with what few children there were and discussed tribal matters with the men. When the orange sun started to set on the horizon, he made his way to the old, green Cadillac where Pansy Sky Walker lived. Her weight prevented her from enjoying a lot of things the other tribal members took for granted, like sitting on the ground cross legged. When Pansy told her stories of the tribe she stood or sat in the driver's seat of her old car and spoke from her seated position there. There were no chairs in the camp except for the built in ones inside the silver bullet shaped travel trailers. Pansy was too wide to get thru the camper doors so she didn't socialize with the tribe's women. Gray Feather knew she had to be as lonely as he was, so he visited last with her every evening and they contemplated the stars and the universe together. They discussed music and philosophy. He had opinions and favorites in the music scene but he didn't know where he had listened to the groups or read the books. He just knew his likes and dislikes. Every night, he asked Pansy to relate to him one of the tribe's stories. He was gaining knowledge of the tribe and how they functioned which helped him to fit in.

Jo Hammers

 Fall was on its way. It was September and the air in the dessert was changing. It was a Monday morning and Gray Feather wondered why the two or three children in the camp weren't in school. Education in the white man's language and ways was not a priority with the Weelo tribe. Some members had an eighth grade education. Somewhere inside himself he knew that he was an educated man. He just couldn't remember where he read books and knew what he knew.

 Each evening when the cool of the day arrived, Pansy Sky Walker would teach the children, as they sat on the hood of her car, the legends and knowledge of the Weelo culture. The tribe had a secret that Gray Feather couldn't figure out. He figured that one day Pansy would tell him what it was. As a medicine man he was sure that he knew the great secret. He just couldn't remember it and was too embarrassed to ask her what it was.

 Breakfast was over and Gray Feather was helping Grandmother Moon Dance to circle the Hogan and spread her sitting rugs for the day. He always made sure she was comfortable and had something to drink sitting next to her before he spread his own sitting rugs on the opposite side of the Hogan for the day.

 "Why aren't the children in school today? It is Monday." He asked her.

 "Today is Gathering Animals Day, Gray Feather. The children will go out into the dessert and bring back two of something. It is practice for when the great Mother Ship comes for us. Each of us must board with a pair of animals or living beings of some sort. We will eat whatever the children bring in today and have a powwow tonight in celebration of the importance of animals to us."

 "I see. . ." he stated cringing at the thought. He ate meat to survive, but he was sure that he did not eat meat in his life before the fog. He knew he had to eat meat to survive in the tribe. The desert was not farming country. He traded his shares of meat for boxes of oatmeal and vegetables when he could. Sometimes, he ate meat because there was nothing else to eat. "Will the animals be killed humanely?"

 "The animals will become human and walk amongst us, Gray Feather. They will move from animal form to becoming part of us. We eat meat to survive here in the dessert. In doing so, the animals live within us and become human."

 "I know that I just live in this body called Gray Feather. I know that the souls of the animals just live in the bodies they travel in. However, who am I to take away their vehicle in which they move and have their being. It would be like taking a way Pansy Sky Walker's old car. Without it she would almost become like a tree planted in one spot bending in the wind but never moving from one land to another." He replied."What if the animals we eat would choose to take away the bodies you and I travel in?"

"I personally, Gray Feather, am tired of this body I travel in and would welcome an animal freeing me from it. You are traveling in a young, handsome, sports car of a body. I am traveling in a vehicle that should have been sent to the salvage yard years ago. I am ready for a new vehicle. The quirk in Earth life is that you don't get a new car body till your old car body dies and gives up the ghost. I would welcome some animal freeing me. I can't seem to free myself."

Gray Feather hugged her shoulders as he helped her sit down on her rug. She was his pet and he took good care of her. She had taken good care of him when he needed it. If he ever married in the tribe, his wife would have to understand that he and Grandmother Moon Dance came as a package deal. Pansy Sky Walker had told him that he was crazy and she definitely would never consider him with another woman in tow. Pansy Sky Walker had not gotten over Grandmother Moon Dance claiming Gray Feather and the tribe going along with it.

After getting the grandmother settled, he walked around the Hogan, spread his rugs and sat down to face his day as a medicine man. A small Indian boy about eight walked up and sat down next to him, crossed his legs, and grinned at Gray Feather waiting for the medicine man to speak first which was their custom.

"What would you inquire of the Great Spirit this morning?" Gray Feather asked straightening his back and grinning at the little boy whose long black hair was loose and hanging down his back. He looked like he had been eating a peanut butter and jelly sandwich. There was purple goo on one side of his face.

"How! My name is Howling Wolf." The boy greeted raising one hand and grinning from ear to ear.

"How!" Gray Feather returned raising one hand like the little boy. Are you Weelo or are you a TV Western Indian?"

"I saw a western that showed us Indians greeting the white men that way. What does how mean?"

"Maybe it is short for how are you today." Gray Feather replied amused.

"Is that what being a man of few words means?" the boy replied. "My teacher said I should quit interrupting class and work on being a man of few words."

"Sometimes speaking briefly is a good thing. What if your mother was disciplining you and she was ranting on and on about what a bad boy you had been and what trouble you were in and how your dad was going to beat your backside when he came home from work? Wouldn't you rather your mother take one brief look at you and say simply, 'Bad!' and go her way?"

"That makes sense. I will explain that to my mother." The boy stated grinning. "She hurts my ears sometimes with her ranting."

Gray Feather continued, "Explain to your father that discipline can be brief as well. Instead of him beating your backside, he could point a finger at you and say, 'Consider your back side beaten.'"

"Thank you Gray Feather. I am definitely a how man."

"I am too. " Gray Feather laughed.

The children of the Weelo tribe were his delights. Even though Pansy was teaching the children not to embrace the white man's ways, the children were very much adopting the white man's culture into their worlds. Gray Feather figured that Howling Wolf's parents possibly had a DVD player in their bullet trailer and were running it off a battery or a generator. The boy was watching westerns somewhere.

"What question do you need answered by the Great Spirit this morning?"

Gray Feather eyed the little raven haired boy who was wearing jeans, tennis shoes, and an action hero T-Shirt. Around his forehead was tied a Harley scarf instead of the traditional Indian head band of leather and feathers. He tried to remember back when he was that age and what his headpiece looked like. Nothing came to him. There were no memories in his fogged brain.

After a moment or so of fidgeting and watching a lizard run past them, the little Indian boy spoke. "A great owl flew into our bullet flyer door this morning thinking it was a barn. It scared my mother big time. I took the broom and swung at the owl causing it to fly back out the door."

One should never kill a bird or animal unless you are very hungry and need it for food." Gray Feather replied.

"I did not kill it. I just scared it like it did my mother."

"One day that owl will come back to haunt you and scare you, possibly in your dreams. Animals and birds don't have brains like us. We must be their protectors. We are the big brains of the Great Spirit's creatures."

"This feather from the owl's tail fell to the floor of our bullet flyer. My mother says the feather is a sign and a gift from the Great Spirit." He stated in an excited and curious voice. He was pleased to have someone listen to his story of the feather even if he was getting somewhat scolded on the mistreatment of creatures.

"Did you knock the Owl's tail feather out accidentally with your broom?" Gray Feather asked.

"No, the owl got away. I think he lost his tail feather when he brushed against the door frame flying out." Howling Wolf replied. "If I had hit him, he would have lost all of his tail feathers. I was a little nervous and my aim wasn't as good as usual with my mother screaming and jumping all over the place."

"If you hurt the owl and caused him to lose his tail feather, it is a bad sign. A curse will fall on your home in the bullet flyer, possibly chicken pox or a bad sore throat. Worse than that, the owl could curse you with a big, fat backside when you are a man and no pretty maiden will want to consider you for a husband. Every Indian man must have a woman to keep his cold feet warm in the winter."

"Really?" The boy questioned big eyed. "Is that why Pansy Sky Walker has an ugly, big backside? Did she hit an owl with a broom when she was little?"

"Only she knows. Why don't you go see her later and ask her? Perhaps if you pointed out her flaw she would lose weight after apologizing to the owl she once hit."

"I will do that. She must be a regular broom swinger at owls to have a back side as large as hers. I will insist she tell me the story."

"Tell Pansy for me that I know about her stash of cookies in the trunk of her car and that she should be dividing them equally between everyone, in particular Grandmother Moon Dance who has no one to watch out for her and see that she has sweets to eat."

"Done!" Howling Wolf stated grinning. Then he asked. "How was that for being a man of few words?"

"The Great Spirit is pleased with you, Howling Wolf. Is there anything else you would like to ask of the Great Spirit.?"

"Dog." He replied grinning.

"I gather Howling Wolf, a man of few words, is asking the Great Spirit for a pet dog? Am I right?"

"Howling Wolf speaks with a straight tongue of few words. I want dog. "

"The Great Spirit is in a bartering or trading mood today. He says you must find one sick animal and care for it for three months. When the three months is up, he will send you a dog."

Jo Hammers

"You mean I have to work for my dog?"

"There will be no dog for you from the Great Spirit till you care for one sick animal. I Gray Feather, medicine man to the Weelo have spoken."

The little Indian boy was big eyed. "What if I cannot find a sick animal? The tribe eats most of the animals that come along."

"If you cannot find a sick animal to care for by noon today, then you must help Pansy Sky Walker to get well. She is one of the Great Spirit's creatures just as dogs and cats are. She is sick from being too fat. You are to knock on her door every morning before you go to school and walk her like a dog. She needs exercise. Three months of walking her will make her start to get better. Then the Great Spirit will send you a dog."

"How far should I walk the dog named Pansy Sky Walker?" Howling Wolf asked.

"A half a mile out into the dessert and then back every morning. Your caring for Pansy Sky Walker will show the Great Spirit that you are able to walk a dog of your own and care for it."

"What if she does a doggy doo-doo on the path, do I have to take along a pooper scooper?"

Caught off guard, Gray Feather snorted and couldn't help but laugh till tears came in his eyes. He loved this kid.

"If Pansy Sky Walker does a doggy doo-doo on the tribe's path, you come get me and I will clean it up." Gray Feather stated after he was able to control himself.

"It is a deal, Gray Feather. I will go home now and tell my mother that I have spoke with you concerning my interrupting class and my wanting a dog. She made me put on this clean shirt before coming. The one I had on was fine with me. It just had a little ketchup and yesterday's grape jelly on it. She was afraid you would think the ketchup was blood. She says you are a vegetable-aria, whatever that means."

Gray Feather laughed and patted the little boy on the back and sent him on his way. Being a medicine man wasn't a bad thing. He was improving human relations and standing up for animal rights. Then he wondered where the words animal rights came from. The words must have come from the Great Spirit because Pansy Sky Walker had assured him that he was who he was. He had no choice but to trust her assurance of all things concerning him. He sure as Hell didn't trust his brain that seemed to be lost in its fog.

"Sure as Hell . . . where did that come from?"He muttered to himself."Do Indians believe in hell? I am sure that I am a Catholic medicine man that believes in hell. Is that possible?"

It was about three in the afternoon when a younger male of the tribe showed up tossing his back pack down on the ground and then plopped down on the rug next to Gray Feather. He was about seventeen and wore glasses which were unusual in the tribe. The tribe avoided all doctors or any professionals of any sort beyond their tribe. Some secret they held kept them aloof and apart from the white man as they called anyone not them. Even the black race was referred to by them as white men.

"I am Gray Feather, your fairly new medicine man. Do you have an inquiry of the Great Spirit this afternoon?"

"I am sorry I am so long in getting here. I have a part time job after school and also work on weekends in town. Tonight is the first night I have had off probably in six months or so. I am saving money for college expenses. I have a full college scholarship, but anything personal expenses I will have to pay. I am getting a head start on some pocket change. "

"I see," Gray Feather stated as the teen stopped a moment to catch his breath."Tell me about your plan."

"I am a modern Weelo and plan to leave the reservation and go to college next fall. This is my senior year and I am counting the days till I am out of here."

"I remember that feeling. I think. You want freedom to stay out past midnight without having to explain where you have been or the time."

"You have it. I make my own money and have earned a scholarship. I have earned the right to some freedom."

"That is acceptable with the Great Spirit. You are a man. Had this been the 1700's you would have been a man at fourteen and would have joined the men on raids. I see you as a man."

"I am here because my father, Walking Snake, has insisted that I come for counseling. He thinks you are the real McCoy, a soul flyer from the Great Mother ship. I don't. You look Italian to me. I have an Italian friend at school whose parents own a spaghetti restaurant. The two of you sound alike and he has a four o'clock shadow at the end of the day like you. "

"What should the Great Spirit and I call you?" Gray Feather asked.

"My name is Road Runner." Replied the teen not the least bit interested in being counseled.

Jo Hammers

"Do you have a question for the Great Sprit?"

"The only thing I am interested in is what I am going to do next weekend. The boss is finally giving me Saturdays off and I am going to sneak out of camp and be young for a change. I have paid my dues."

Out of nowhere, Gray Feather had a flash of himself being a teen playing a guitar. He jumped to his feet and started singing and pretending to pick a hard rock guitar.

"May the bird of Para-something fly up your . . . nose . . . nose . . . nose . . . !" Then he made a dip with his invisible guitar and ran some invisible pretend chords up and down the instrument's neck. He jumped up and down pointing the neck of the guitar up and then down like he was moving to the rhythm of a frenzied rock beat. "May the secret I'm going home with burn my nose . . . nose . . . nose." Then he stopped and wondered where he had learned to play the guitar. In the flash of memory, he saw himself on a stage jamming it. He wondered where the memory came from and why he had only a three second flash of it come back to him. He didn't see a location for the event, only flashing blinding lights on a stage. "It is better to have a flash memory as no memory at all.' He muttered. "Maybe I am getting better in the head. Maybe my memory is going to come back." He muttered extremely happy about the flash.

The seventeen year old Indian boy had stood in a panic when his medicine man went into his night club act. When Gray Feather opened his eyes and stopped playing his pretend guitar, the boy in shock asked. "Who told you that I have been playing secretly in a white man's band on the weekends called the PARA SOME THINGS?"

"I guess the Great Spirit," Gray Feather replied. "I gather your parents do not know?"

"They believe rock music is vibrations that are interfering with communications with Great Mother Ship and the ancient ones. They are naïve and lost in worship of Weelo fables. Religion is full of fables and falsehoods that cause men to live less than they could be. None of our tribe has pursued their special talents because the tribe's religion tells them they must wait for the mother ship to return. They will die old with their music still in them. I want more than that. I am a musician and just want to play my guitar with my friends on the weekend till I go off to college. I am not goofing off or selling my soul to the kachina. I am a 4.0 student with a full music scholarship to college. I just want a little freedom to be young and enjoy my white buddies. I am not dumb. I know that when high school is over, some of my friends I will probably never see again because we are all heading off in different directions. I am headed for New Jersey to go to col-

70

lege."

"New Jersey?" Gray Feather asked rolling the words over in his mind. The land of New Jersey sounded so familiar. Maybe it was just the Great Spirit showing him that the teen would be okay there. "I feel the Great Spirit is telling me it is okay for you to use your talents in the land of New Jersey. Also, I will speak with your mother concerning the weekends. Send her to me for a counseling session at my request tomorrow. Tell her the Great Spirit has sent me a message for her."

"Our Indian ways are miserable for the younger members of the tribe to live with. We have been to school and have seen the many conveniences the white man uses and know that we are perfectly able to work and better ourselves. There is no Great Mother Ship coming, Gray Feather. The Weelo tribe has waited for thousands of years for this ship to come. It's a cop out, a way of keeping the Weelo people in isolation and self imposed poverty. I want more. My younger brother, Howling Wolf would make a great pet store owner or a veterinarian. He is crazy about animals. My parents won't even let him have a dog. He has music in him that possibly will never be played. His talent for healing and caring for animals will go to his grave with him. I am a rebellion. I got out and found myself a job and decided I was having a high school education with or without my parent's approval. I am hard headed enough to create a means of putting myself thru college. "

"I will not tell your parents about the Para Some Things Band and see to it that your younger brother goes on to high school and college if you will do something for me."

"Are you suggesting black mail with benefits?" Road Runner asked.

"The Great Spirit always rewards cooperation." Gray Feather replied.

"Alright, lay it on me. What do you want to keep you quiet about the PARA-SOMETHINGS and for seeing that my brother is able to get an education?"

"Pansy Sky Walker has forgotten how to sing. Her music as a story teller is in her and will die with her. Should she lose weight and embrace a white lifestyle, she could become a famous Weelo Indian historian putting the tribe's legends in a readable book. Unless we help her, she will probably be dead within a year."

"She is a half breed, Gray Feather, and has no goals. She is a waste of time."

"I want you to take her with you to the club where you are playing on the weekends and dance with her till the fat starts to drop off of her. I am asking for four Saturday nights of Dancing with Pansy Sky Walker as your date."

Jo Hammers

"But she is . . . ," Road Runner sputtered not finishing his sentence.

"Yes, she is big, ugly, and fat in your eyes. You must look in her and see the great writer that is hidden within her. You must show her that there is life out there and she is not too big or ill to enjoy it. Otherwise, I will go Sunday morning and tell your parents that the Kachina has your soul in their clutches and that your baby brother is to drop out of school when he turns sixteen."

"Four Saturday nights and no more!" yelled the Road Runner in disgust at being blackmailed. "What makes you think she can dance? She can hardly shuffle her feet across the dessert to the full moon camp fire."

"Her shuffle will turn to jogging and dancing in six month's time. She is the voice of your people, the keeper of the legends. You will be a legend. You would hate for her not to be around to pass down your successes in the music business as part of the tribe's history. One day you will grow old and pass away just like the old people we have now like Hissing Cat. Some future Indian child that you will not know may need the story teller's words about a tribe member named Road Runner who was a perfect student as well as a college educated musician who went on to be famous and wrote sound tracks for movies. It would be a shame if an Indian boy like you was never given an idol to encourage him to become all he could be and go to live in the land of the Whites if necessary."

"I am going to be famous?" the Road Runner asked suddenly interested in the medicine man's words.

"Only if you make a bargain with the Great Spirit and dance Pansy Sky Walker's butt off for the next four Saturday nights and not let her have any sugar or possum fat."

"I do have to think long term, don't I? Tell the Great Spirit that I will do it."

Gray Feather smiled. "You will not regret this Road Runner. Pansy Sky Walker will be famous also."

"Stars have to stick together," replied the teen. "I now see Pansy in a new light. I will form a friendship with her and make sure my name is in her head and heart."

"The Great Spirit is pleased. Tell your parents that they are to take turns sitting on my rug the Sunday after your four Saturdays of taking Pansy dancing."

"You can count on me, Gray Feather. I just knew I was going to be famous someday."

Road Runner rose and left after leaving a banana in the medicine man's basket. It had been part of his school lunch earlier in the day. He hadn't found the time

72

to eat it.

Gray Feather was really pleased with the banana. He rose from his position and walked around to the back of the Hogan and split it with the Grandmother whom he was sure wasn't getting enough fruits and vegetables in her diet. She was his pet and her needs were equal to his. He loved her and always gave her the larger half of anything he had.

CHAPTER NINE

THE SINGING WOLF

A year had passed and it was once more the Christmas season although the Weelo didn't celebrate it. Gray Feather was lonely, but reluctant to enter a permanent relationship with any of the Weelo women. He feared that he might have a wife and children lost somewhere in his brain fog. Occasionally, the name Carol came to him but no face to go with it. Desperate and lonely, he had made up his mind to discuss the matter with Grandmother Moon Dance. There was no elder medicine man or chief to discuss the matter with. Grandfather Night Shadow, who was showing signs of the onset of dementia, had no interest in counseling the tribe anymore. Gray Feather had taken over Night Shadows duties as tribal medicine man. The chief of the tribe had died before Gray Feather arrived. Grandmother Moon Dance was now head of the tribe till the Weelo chose a new chief which was probably going to be a forty year old man named Three Toes. There was a social pecking order in the tribe and you didn't ask advice from anyone below your position in the tribe. Grandmother Moon Dance was in a higher position than him, so that was his choice to discuss his loneliness and desire for a woman with. If he wanted a Weelo woman, he had to go thru her. That was just the way it was.

After breakfast on Christmas Eve morning, Gray Feather got up the courage to ask counseling from Grandmother Moon Dance concerning his loneliness and his fears that he might have a wife and children somewhere. The morning clean-up of the breakfast dishes was over. He took a deep breath as he dried the last fork and then hung his wet tea towel to dry. Talking about sex with your doctor he didn't see as a problem. However, his doctor was a woman and his best friend in the tribe. He didn't want to be seen as a man whose brain was in his yang and thought from there. He took a second deep breath and started a conversation with her.

"Do you have time to put me on your list of tribe members to counsel today? I have a serious physical problem needing a remedy. It has to do with my heart."

"A problem of the heart…? She questioned grinning.

"Yes! My brain in its fog is dead, but other parts of me are not. I have a problem. "

"You will be first to sit on my rug this morning. I have known for days that you have been trying to get up the courage to speak with me concerning something. Help me out of the Hogan and around to my sitting rugs and we will talk. Make sure you have a chocolate payment for my services with you."

Gray Feather grinned. He wondered if she knew how much he loved her. Also, he knew that she had got up in the middle of the night and ate the chocolate bar he was saving to pay her with. Grandmother Moon Dance had a thing for chocolate. She just couldn't resist it. Sometimes he hid his chocolate just so she would find it and be tempted.

"I have my payment ready and I am not going to tell you what dark hole it is in till after you counsel me. I wouldn't want you drooling over it and giving me a half hearted counsel in an effort to obtain payment quickly."

"That is probably wise, Gray Feather. I am a woman and you know why females like myself love chocolate. It is a stress reliever and living with two jackass medicine men requires a lot of chocolate."

"Who says it is a chocolate bar? Maybe it is a bag of Pansy Sky Walker's cookies or a candy cane given Howling wolf at the Bell Ringer's annual Christmas party for poor Indian Children."

"I know it is chocolate. A little mouse was up last night and sampled one corner of it and then the other three corners. The center looked so lonely that the mouse ate it to so it could join the four corners in the mouse's warm stomach. The center didn't want to be left out in the cold." She replied grinning.

"You ate my chocolate bar?" he asked folding his arms across his chest like he was annoyed. He had saved it for her from his payment basket. He shared anything that was good with her. Occasionally, he got a pet Tarantula or lizard left in payment which he turned loose.

"I didn't eat it. The night mouse did." She replied folding her arms and grinning. "Would you deny a mouse a Christmas Eve treat? "

"Christmas Eve . . ." he muttered like there was some memory that was trying to come to him. As hard as he tried, he couldn't pull the memory up.

"Last night was the white man's Christmas Eve and his mouse, the one not stirring in the story about the night before Christmas, awoke and came for your chocolate bar."

"You should be the story teller for the tribe, not Pansy Sky Walker. What am I going to pay you with now?" he asked amused.

"You will think of something. Come to my rug ten minutes after I sit down there. I need a few minutes to speak with the Great Spirit about a mouse in my house that likes chocolate belonging to others."

"I think that ten minutes of penance is a good thing. How did you find my hiding place?" he asked loving his interaction with her and still trying to recall what it was about Christmas Eve that was trying to come back to him. The only thing he could recall was him jumping into the back of some sort of truck. What he remembered was fuzzy and brief.

"I am a great medicine woman with magical ears and eyes. I know all. You cannot hide anything from me, Gray Feather. I know you inside and out."

"I wish I was so fortunate. I don't know me on the inside or in the past. Could you loan me your magical ears and eyes?"

"Help me to my rug, Gray Feather. I already know what your problem is. You are lonely and desire one of our young maidens to sleep with, but you fear you have a wife and children somewhere lost in your brain fog."

"Shit, Moon Dance." He cursed without thinking."Are you a mind reader or something? Do you know what it is like to live in a lodge with a medicine woman who always knows what you are thinking? Suppose I should have thoughts about having intimate relations with some maiden, would you listen in just because you can read me like a book?"

"I saved you from death. I claimed you in front of the tribe. I have the right to listen in on your soul thoughts."She replied grinning from ear to ear. She loved him as much as he loved her. He filled her lonely hours which should have been filled by her sons. Four of her five sons had died drunk in a car wreck heading home from a white man's bar. Her one remaining son was a truck driver and one of the tribe's providers. He was rarely home. Her only daughter had deserted the tribe, embraced the white man's world, and had become a social worker.

"You just wait. I am going to think something tonight that will be really off the wall and intimate just so you will have to blush and tune me out."

"I am a medicine woman, Gray Feather. I have heard it all."

"Good point, I will have to think hard to come up with something that you haven't heard."

"I will be listening in, surprise me. Make me blush."

Gray Feather looked at her and laughed. He could never get the best of her and he loved her for loving him. He didn't know what he would do without her. She was his sunshine in the morning and the last person he said good night to when the moon was in the sky. He loved her more than Pansy Sky Walker, but he would never tell her that. She would be appalled if she knew he sometimes fantasized about her lying next to him and keeping him warm like she did when he was so ill. He would like to repeat the moment but he didn't dare ask her for that or even admit wanting it. He felt really safe the night she lay and held him. The wanting of her to hold him like a little boy was perverted and he wasn't about to give into it. There were certain boundaries as a man that you didn't cross. He was sure he had a screw loose that he had never realized was there.

Gray Feather helped her get settled on her rug behind the Hogan and then walked out into the dessert for a few moments alone to think and give her time for penance. It was going to be really embarrassing to have to discuss dating and sex with her. He was dreading it. However, it was necessary. He was lonely and you had to ask the tribe elder before considering any woman in the tribe. Some were promised to various members. Three Toes as a future chief had four promised to him to choose from. They would be off limits to him.

He had decided to choose a woman in the tribe who did not want to marry. A casual relationship would protect the wife and children he might have that were lost to him in his fog. He could go home to them if his memory ever returned. He was going to ask Grandmother Moon Dance for permission to sleep beneath the quilt of Running Deer who was a dedicated Weelo. She was ten years older than him and was rumored to have slept her way from one coast to the other as a truck driver turning down and laughing at all offers of marriage. He had given it some long, hard thought.

Gray Feather thought about Pansy Sky Walker for a moment. He felt bad about not considering her. She was not in the best of health and had weak lungs from Asthma. He was sure that she would die of a heart attack from spending one night with him as lonely as he was. In his mind, he knew he was going to be an animal from having not been with a woman in so long. Pansy couldn't handle that. He felt really bad for not choosing her because he did have feelings for her. He didn't know how he was going to explain his choice to her without being blunt and he was not willing to go there. She was going to feel rejected and be one pissed Indian woman. Even worse, Running Deer was the mother who had never wanted her and abandoned her to whichever tribe member that was willing to care for her when she was little. Pansy was going to see him as a traitor and a man rejecting her.

Gray Feather walked back from the desert and seated himself on the rug next to Grandmother Moon Dance, crossed his legs, and waited for her to speak first which was the Weelo custom. She was the medicine woman, he was the rug sitter.

"I assume you have come to speak with me about the birds and the bees?" Grandmother Moon Dance asked grinning from ear to ear."Aren't you a little old to need the talk?"

Gray Feather blushed as he turned and looked at her. She was purposely ribbing him. He could see a mischievous sparkle in her dark brown, almost black eyes. She seemed to know how to push all of his buttons.

"I am a young buck and would have asked Grandfather Night Shadow to counsel me, but it seems a young medicine man who has taken his place now on the rugs in front of the Hogan. I wish to be counseled by a more experienced doctor than him. I do hope you are older than the new medicine man and know about the birds and the bees! You couldn't be a day over nineteen in my thinking. Perhaps, I should wait for an older medicine man in the tribe to come along to hear me."

Grandmother Moon Dance beamed. "I think this nineteen year old medicine woman is capable of curing any problem you might have as well as give you the long overdue talk about the heart that runs like a deer and the snake that hisses. What is your question for the Great Spirit this morning?"

"I am considering asking for a woman to share my bed. However, my heart doesn't race for her. It is the hissing snake that is the problem. I feel there is possibly a woman who existed before my brain fog set in. I am not sure I want children or marriage for that reason."

"I assume you are familiar with the use of male items to prevent pregnancies?" She asked grinning from ear to ear and biting her lip.

"Those items have been dropped in my payment basket occasionally by the wives of some of our tribe members as hints of availability. I have not used them, but I admit that I have been tempted by one tribe member's wife in particular."

"Is she your age?" Grandmother Moon Dance asked frowning and wondering what young tribal member's wife had her eye on Gray Feather. She had heard no confession from anyone sitting on her sitter's rug.

"I cannot answer that question since I don't know how old I am. Because of my brain fog I am one year old. That is how many years of memories I have. I would have to say that she is indeed older than me."He replied loving that she was fishing for information.

"It is my duty as the tribe's medicine woman to warn you that a medicine man becomes an old fart and fool if he chooses one who is too young for him. You are at least thirty in my thinking and I know that our sixteen year old maiden named Wind Song has a crush on you. Young maidens eventually run away with young bucks and the old fart sleeps alone in his old age with no one to warm his cold feet on."

"It is not Wind Song that I am interested in. I would like to sing the wolf's song beneath the moon with a woman nearer the age you say that I am. She is as lonely as I am, I think. I have no intentions of being an old fart and I am willing to mate with a widow, divorcee, or a woman with a colorful past. I am not a young medicine man anymore. Looking at my body and considering my brain fog, I am not a prize for any Indian woman to take on. I will not disrespect myself or you by being an old fart. I will be a wise medicine man and take your advice as to who I should consider."

"I am pleased to know that you are wise enough not to be an old fart. Are you wise enough not to be a thirty year old fool is the question?" She replied.

"What do you mean?" he asked.

"One should never mate unless it is for love. Hot handsome and beautiful bodies get tired and old. Hearts can hold each other's hand for eternity. A thirty year old fart might settle for a hot bed, but miss out on arms to love him that will one day come along. When that special one shows up, would a wise thirty year old medicine man want to be tied to the bed of another?"

"That is a good point, Grandmother Moon Dance. Suppose the right one has already shown up and I cannot remember her? Suppose somewhere out there in the fog I have a wife and children looking for me that I don't remember? Most men my age are married."

"If that is your feeling, you should not consider another. It would be disrespecting the current woman you wish to share a bed with. Two wives or more are for the men who live in the land of Utah. Perhaps you should go and practice medicine there where it is acceptable? It is not acceptable in this medicine woman's eyes."

"How do I put this?" he stated pausing for a moment. "I love a woman here, but she is not able to love me. Pansy Sky Walker is not well enough to sleep with me. I have been alone here for a year and have the desires of a man. The wild, caged animal in me could cause Pansy to have a heart attack and die the first time we went beyond the lover's dune of sand. The only other woman I love is you and you are much too young for me at nineteen. Plus, Grandfather Night Shadow

79

might put a hatchet in my skull. I was thinking that there might be a woman in the tribe who doesn't wish to ever marry and would agree to a no strings to the bed attachment?"

"How much in love are you with Pansy Sky Walker?" she asked with a sudden sadness and loneliness in her eyes and the smile disappearing from her face. She thought about Night Shadow and his disrespect of her as his wife and how her own heart ran like a deer for someone she couldn't have because she was chained to the grandfather.

"I am lonely, Grandmother Moon Dance. I do have feelings for Pansy but I cannot sleep with her. She has serious health issues and I am sure that she is going to die if she doesn't continue to lose weight. She is not up to strenuous activity for now and that includes making love. An accidental pregnancy could put too much stress on her body. This animal would not be a good thing for her."

"You are indeed in a fog, Gray Feather. I don't think you could recognize love if it bit you like a rattlesnake on your backside. Two hearts that love each other stands by each other in the good and the bad times. This is Pansy's bad time and you are thinking of sleeping with someone else. In my current thinking as a medicine woman, you are a young version of Grandfather Night Shadow, a man who does not cling tightly to the one in good and bad. Your brain is in your snake and not in your heart where it should be. One day, you might be sorry for choosing casually for a hot bed. However, I am willing to let you have your folly. Do you have someone in the tribe in mind who has been dropping birth control items your payment basket?"

"The woman I am possibly choosing is not the one who has been doing the dropping. I thought perhaps Running Deer might be the answer to my problem. It is rumored that she has slept with many in her semi truck as she has traveled across the country as a provider and is not picky. I am no prize. I have an almost dead brain in a fog." He stated swallowing and expecting the grandmother to hit him with something. She did take her broom or dish towel to him occasionally.

"What about your conversion to the Catholic religion and its belief that you can have only one woman for a lifetime?"

"I am wrestling with my beliefs. Somehow, I know that I am a vegetarian. I have wrestled with that because there have been times here in the dessert that meat is all we have to eat. I have eaten meat to survive, to live. Would sleeping with someone to survive be any different? I am so lonely and I have a man's desires. I think I am going to go crazy if I don't sleep with a woman soon." He stated and then really blushed. Putting his fingers together, he popped his knuckles like a little kid having had to confess to something.

"I am an old woman, Gray Feather. In my years of counseling the younger men and women of the tribe, I have heard it all. I know what it is to be lonely and want a partner in your bed. I chose unwisely when I was young. There was only one single man in the tribe near my age and of equal status in the Weelo tribe being a medicine man. I chose Grandfather Night Shadow thinking we were compatible. We were both medicine men. There was no racing of the heart. However, sex was good. We were young and proud of our decision to be able to choose. Now that we are old, he says I am not an appealing woman anymore. He wants untied from my bed saying I have stood in his way my whole life preventing him from mating with Hissing Cat who came along after we were married. He has always compared me to her and saw our children as ropes around his neck. He is right. We are tied to the marriage bed with a chosen mate instead of the hand in hand one meant for us."

"Is that why you and Hissing Cat are always at odds with each other?"

"She spent years with a chief that chose her because the man she was intended for was married to me. She sees my children as ones that should have been born to her. All of her children by the chief either died young, at birth, or were still born. She is childless to care for her in her old age. She would like to take you from me to get even. She sees how you spoil me with chocolate bars and all the good things from your payment basket. She does not see me as worthy of it."

"You are worthy of it, Grandmother Moon Dance. I would have died the day I arrived here if it hadn't been for your caring for me. You own part of me that will never belong to any other woman. You earned that part of me. Hissing Cat cannot take that part of me from you. That part of me will always walk hand in hand with you."

"You please me, Gray Feather, with your words. You are human, but you may hold on to my braid when the Great Mother Ship arrives. I will make sure you are able to board with me, providing you don't ask me to let you bring along a chosen woman. I am not taking Night Shadow with me and I will not be taking a woman you have chosen on board either."

"I get your point, Grandmother Moon Dance. You have made your feelings clear about an old fart medicine man and a young brainless one named Gray Feather." He replied seeing the sadness in her eyes.

"Grandfather Night Shadow wants to be chief. He is doing everything in his power to keep Three Toes from becoming the respected leader of our tribe. He cannot marry Hissing Cat as long as I am alive because I stand in the way. He is not crazy with dementia as many think. He is just tired of me and our life to-gether and is waiting and hoping for me to die. I should set his boots outside my door and divorce him. You do know that divorce is the woman's choice here, not the man's. He can only be free from me if I choose to sit his boots outside the door or if I die. He is a dark soul human and I am protecting the human Weelo tribe by not divorcing him. I have nothing against Hissing Cat. If I hadn't chosen Night Shadow before she came along, she would have possibly been fooled by him and married him becoming a medicine man's wife. Hissing Cat, when she was young, was the most gorgeous creature every known to our tribe. Night Shadow wanted her but he was already married to me. She was not the hand in hand heart of the chief either. She was status to him, being so beautiful. She will not admit that she settled like me for a chosen human mate. We are alike being true Weelo of the stars. We both got weary in our waiting and chose to mate and have human families. Now the times is coming when we must leave the humans we have mated with and the offspring that we have loved behind. You, I do not wish to leave behind. Choose well, Gray Feather. Life becomes hard and your heart forgets to run like a deer if you make bad choices."

"Would just sleeping with Running Deer with no attachments be so bad? I understand what you are saying to me, but the human man in me wants a woman and I think Carol is waiting for me out there in the fog somewhere. I remember the name but not her face."

"I will send Running Deer to sit on your rug tomorrow. If you can work out the situation with her with no rope attachments, I will turn my head. However, don't ask me for another woman in the same fashion because I will not agree to it. One chance with one woman to sing like a wolf beyond the dune is all you will be granted. If Pansy Sky Walker is the heart you wish to hold hands with, you are misguided in not waiting for her to lose weight and get healthy. I am actually ashamed of you Gray Feather in your asking of another. In your brain fog, you are indeed thinking with the brain of your hissing snake."

"Damn it, Grandmother Moon Dance. It hasn't been my intention to get on your list of jackasses."

"Pay up, Jackass, your counseling session is over."

"The Hogan mouse has already eaten my chocolate bar. I guess you will have to settle for my going into the Hogan and making you a glass of tea and bringing it out to you."

"That is agreeable! Bring me a corn cake also with a little honey on it. I am having a chocolate stress morning and need a woman's cure all. Damn that mouse that ate the chocolate bar last night!"

"The mouse won't eat it the next time, I have thought up a new hiding place."

He stated hugging her shoulders. The request to sleep with running deer had lost its appeal to him because he knew he was on the Grandmother's list of jackass men. He didn't mind when Pansy, the tribe, or Night Shadow were mad at him. She was a different story. He didn't want to look little in her eyes or her heart.

Leaning in where no one could hear him, he whispered, "I will control the snake. You are right. I will wait for my brain fog to clear to see who Carol is. I am old enough to make better decisions. It is a good thing I have you to keep my head on straight and the snake asleep."

Grandmother Moon Dance turned her face to him, smiled and then kissed him on his cheek.

"Now, get up and go get my tea. Spank the paws of that mouse if you catch her eating our chocolate again. I really need that bar this morning. She was a bad mouse."

Two years passed. Gray Feather kept his word and waited, although there were times when he questioned his decision. He had traded his services as a medicine man to all of the tribe members secretly in exchange for them walking and exercising Pansy Walker for a month or two each. Pansy assumed she was becoming popular amongst the tribe because everyone was asking to walk with her, take her dancing, hunting, fishing, whatever Gray Feather could bargain for. She was being walked at least three times a day for two miles and she was losing weight. She had lost a total of two hundred pounds and was down to somewhere around a hundred and eighty. Part of her breathing problems had gone away. Gray Feather hoped in the next year to see her drop another fifty or so pounds which would bring her down to around a hundred and thirty and into a healthy weight range. He planned to approach Grandmother Moon Dance about seeing her when she did. His brain fog had not cleared and he still didn't know who Carol was. He had come to the conclusion that his brain fog was permanent. He was going to ask Grandmother Moon Dance for permission to marry Pansy when the third year anniversary of his arriving came about. He was dreading asking for Pansy just like he had dreaded asking to sleep with Running Deer.

It was Christmas Eve and there had been several callers to the Hogan from the do-gooders of the town bringing Christmas baskets to the poor Indians. Each had literature from their church and tried to entice a member of the tribe or two to visit their various religious sanctuaries. Gray Feather was a little annoyed because several walked right up and interrupted his counseling sessions as he sat with various members of the tribe needing questions answered. When the last was gone, he started to rise when he saw one last sitter heading his way. Grandmother Moon Dance eased her seventy-plus year old body down on the sitter rug and sat waiting.

"It is Christmas Eve, Grandmother Moon Dance. Are we having a celebration feast from the baskets of goodies the men of town religions have brought us?"

"There is chocolate in the baskets and that is what I have come to talk to you about. I am afraid that I am not capable of dividing it fairly with everyone. I have a problem. I am a pig when it comes to chocolate. Ask the Great Spirit what I am to do?" she asked with a grin on her partly toothless face.

"I think the wise thing to do would be to ask someone who has no sweet tooth to divide the sweets and then ask to trade him your share of something else for his share of chocolate. That way you will get two portions of the chocolate plus mine if I don't keep it hidden well. In fairness you will come out ahead of the others in the long run."

"You are a wise man, Gray Feather. Please hide your share well so the mouse in your house will have chocolate for a long time."

Gray Feather reached over and put his arm around her shoulders and hugged her grinning. He was nuts about her. He loved and wanted Pansy, but he loved Grandmother Moon Dance more. He didn't know why. He just did and was sure that Pansy would be appalled when he told her that Moon Dance would live with them should they marry.

"How many of our tribe converted to the white man's religions today?" he asked seeing she had no further questions for him.

Rock Lizard has agreed to attend the Baptists for now. They have monthly church dinners and will send someone for him. His children need the vegetables. They will all fill their plates strictly with vegetables and bring them home to eat. It is a good conversion for the winter months. His children will have the vitamins they need plus the Baptists have a food pantry. The children will have cereal and other items to eat that are kid friendly. Being Baptist for the winter is a good thing."

"Has anyone else converted for the winter?" he asked amused.

"Pansy Sky Walker has joined the door knockers. They stop for lunch on Saturdays at Mc Dees. It is a free trip to town once a week for her and fast food. They will come pick her up. She will carry their literature in exchange for a free meal. They will feel sorry for her because she has no money for lunch and pay for hers."

"So, my Pansy is going to be a door knocker?" he asked once more amused. He was going to have to talk to Pansy about getting herself a part time job now that she had lost weight and being an independent woman who could support herself. He didn't see charity as healthy for the tribe. They were almost con artists in their yearly conversions.

"Your Pansy has been Baptist, Methodist, Lutheran, and now a door knocker."

"Wouldn't it be more practical if the tribe were trained for various occupations and worked for food and clothing? They could live much better lives and give back to society instead of sucking what they can get which takes up just as much time?"

"We are hidden here in the dessert and the US government leaves us alone. We do not take food stamps, welfare, or get jobs requiring us to have IDs and pay taxes. Our children are born and raised without birth certificates and identities known to Uncle Sam. If we need an identity card for some reason, we buy it just like the criminals do in the big cities. The Great Mother Ship will come for us soon and we must keep its arrival and who we are a secret. Government men snooping around might invoke a full out attack on the mother ship. Alone here in the dessert, it can come for us and leave without anyone knowing. We cannot endanger the Mother Ship by inviting trouble. Converting is our way of supplementing out supplies once a year. We convert at Thanksgiving and the churches give us baskets of food and clothing from their pantries as Christmas Charity."

"I know that I am Catholic, Grandmother Moon Dance. Did I convert before my brain fog and failed to convert back after my first Christmas Eve here?"

"It is not a problem, Gray Wolf. Being a Catholic Indian man is a good thing. Any man who embraces religion has his face turned toward the Great Spirit and lives a better life than a non religious man. The members of our tribe who are true converts to the white man's religions live better lives than those who embrace nothing."

"Have you ever converted?" He asked her.

"Three Toes was converted to being a Pentecostal ten years ago. It has taken me nine years to halfway convert him back. He still gets the heebie-jeebies once in a while. He says it is the Holy Ghost moving on him. It jumped off on me once and I did the heebie-jeebies. If I was not a Weelo medicine woman and spiritual leader of our tribe, I might convert to being a follower of the Holy Ghost. I like a Great Spirit that can make you dance around campfires with a hot spirit in your bones. My bones are old and need a little fire in them. Three Toes tells me that the Holy Ghost puts fire in him. The Holy Ghost must be a good spirit."

"You will have to tell me more about the heebie- jeebie fire. Perhaps I need Pen-

Jo Hammers

tecostal fire in my bones. My sleeping rug gets cold this time of year. If you do convert to being a Pentecostal, may I sleep next to you on your rug so I can enjoy some of the heebie-jeebie heat? I was cold last night beneath my quilt."

"You have a lot to learn, Gray Feather. If you are cold at night, crawl under my quilt and warm yourself on my backside. I own you. I saved your life and you are mine. You may use my body for warmth, if I offer it. There is a mouse in our Hogan that has been cold at night, also. Perhaps you should crawl in and warm her backside."

"Are you telling me that I can crawl in your bed and warm myself?"

"Yes."

"Am I like an outside dog that you let in on a freezing cold winter night?"

"I own you. You are my pet and you may crawl in my bed and warm yourself if the winter nights are too uncomfortable for you." She replied.

"Damn it Grandmother Moon Dance. There have been many nights the last two years I have been cold and wished to snuggle up to someone's backside. Why are you telling me this now?"

"I have had to train my outside dog to want to sleep next to me in my bed."

Gray Feather grinned. "I will tell you right now, I am not freezing my buns off tonight. You have the backside of your bed warmed and ready for this dog."

"I need you, Gray Feather. I am old and may need a walking stick soon. I will welcome the heat from your body. I too was cold last night."

"I will always be whatever you need me to be, Moon Dance. I love you more than you will ever know. The greatest Christmas gift I have ever been given is you. You gave yourself to me in the form of caring and healing two years ago when I was so ill, and you still give yourself to me in whatever from I need you. You are a treasure, a gift from the Great Spirit. I love you like no other woman."

So, Doctor Michael Haven or Gray Feather entered a new experience in life, the sleeping with another human being to warm your body and not for sex. Sleeping snuggled to Moon Dance's backside he came to understand why kittens and puppies slept on top of each other and cuddled up with each other. He experienced for himself that pleasure in the warmth of Grandmother Moon Dance's body. He crawled beneath her sleeping blanket on Christmas Eve of his second year as a Weelo medicine man. Grandfather night Shadow ignored them like communal winter sleeping was a common occurrence. He preferred to have a tribe dog named yellow paws sleep with him and keep him warm.

Doctor Michael Haven or Gray Feather fell more in love with the woman who had saved him and now warmed him. By spring, he wasn't sure whether he loved Pansy Sky Walker like he once had. He had become addicted to sleeping cuddled up to the back of Moon Dance and he wasn't sure he wanted to sleep in another woman's bed. Grandmother Moon Dance had become like the pillow that you can't sleep without when you go on vacation. She was part of who he was.

When the heat of spring and summer arrived, much to his dismay, Grandmother Moon Dance kicked him out of her bed and sent him back to sleep beneath the kitchen window on a rug on the ground. It took weeks for him to adjust to sleeping alone again. He missed his pillow.

CHAPTER TEN

THREE TOES

Two years and six months passed. It was the first of July when Gray Feather was surprised to find Three Toes the future Weelo Chief sitting waiting for him on the sitter rug. Usually, Three Toes inquired of Grandmother Moon Dance when he had a problem. This was a first and Gray Feather was excited about having someone besides women asking about birth control to counsel. Sometimes, the men of the tribe were just as bad. They would sit wanting him to ask the Great Sprit to let them shoot a deer bigger than the other men in the tribe which was status. He was ready for some intelligent conversation about anything besides birth control and deer hunting. Three Toes, having traveled in his semi truck beyond the reservation, had more knowledge than the others.

Gray Feather sat down and crossed his legs. "What would you ask of the Great Spirit?" he inquired using the same conversation question he always used to spark a sharing of words.

The tall, physically fit, handsome Indian man with waist long loose hair took out a pack of cigarettes and tapped it on his knee causing a cigarette to forward. He then offered it to Gray Feather who turned it down. There was one oddity about Three Toes. His left boot was handmade and extremely wide across the toe area like a round saucer. On his other foot was a normal western boot.

"I have not come for advice, Gray Feather. I get enough of that from everyone in the tribe. Grandmother Moon Dance tells me that she plans to take you aboard the Great Mother Ship when it comes. That is a great honor. Are your intentions honorable toward the grandmother?"

"Honorable? I don't understand what you are asking." Gray Feather replied.

"Night Shadow tells me you have been sleeping in her bed. He also has told me he wants a divorce which is impossible if the woman says no. He is hoping she will fall in love with you, want to marry you, and will set his boots outside the door. He has been looking for a way for years to get out of his marriage to her."

"She invited me to her bed to warm myself. We are not having sex, if that is your question."

"An older woman is a far better lover than a young woman. However, Night Shadow wants a young wife. I would not blame Grandmother Moon Dance if she chose again and set the grandfather's boots outside the Hogan. He has been playing around on her for a long time. He has a child by one of the younger women that Grandmother Moon Dance does not know about. I have just about had my fill of his ways. When I become chief, I plan to ban him from the tribe. He is an old pervert, not a man of honor."

"Are you asking me to stay out of Moon Dance's Bed?"

We, as a tribe, take care of our old ones. We do it by marrying them and keeping them in our home in a place of respect. We have two older women in the tribe and both will need someone to care for them. You and I are the high ranking members of the Weelo tribe and it will be up to us to each take one of the women. If you have feelings for Moon Dance, I will take Hissing Cat into my trailer and she will become my wife till she passes on to join those with the Great Spirit. You will be expected to take one of the two when Night Shadow is banned from the tribe. I have come to ask you which woman you might feel a preference for?"

"On . . .," Gray Feather replied in shock. "You are doing some pre- planning for when you take over as chief."

"I guess that is one way of looking at it. My plan is to take one of our two elder women. I am asking you to plan to do the same. It is a matter of respect in the tribe. That is why I am asking you if your intentions toward Moon Dance are honorable. In marrying her, you will not be allowed another wife till she crosses over. Rumor has it that you have been seeing Pansy Sky Walker and that she expects you to marry her. I need to know where you stand on this issue. I have very little time in off the road. Driving a truck leaves me little time to piddle around with decisions that need to be made. I need your decision between the two women here and now."

"I love Grandmother Moon Dance more than life itself. She has been there for me in sickness and on cold nights. She has cooked for me and washed my clothes and loved me in spite of my brain fog. There is no decision to be made. I choose Moon Dance. There was a time that I thought I was in love with Pansy Sky Walker. That time is no more. Tonight, I will tell Pansy of my decision to marry Moon Dance and cease calling on her. I will be faithful to Moon Dance."

"The tribe tells me you are a good man. They respect you. I now respect you to. There are many of our young bucks who would not consider marrying Hissing

Cat or Moon Dance seeing them as old, leathered, and ugly. It takes a respectable honorable man to see them for what they are, treasures of the tribe."

"I have struggled with my feelings for Mood Dance, Three Toes. I actually love Moon Dance like a man loves a woman. I have secretly struggled seeing myself as a pervert with a screw loose. Now you are telling me it is okay to love her and it is an honor to marry one of the older women. I could kiss you, but you would probably take a hatchet to me. I want Moon Dance."

"I will speak with Moon Dance telling her of the grandfather's problem and ask her to set his boots out. The night of the powwow when I become chief, we will both declare our intentions of who we will marry. It will be expected of us as part of the ceremony. With Night Shadow out of the picture, you will be next in line to me. Wild Cat, Night Shadow and Moon Dance's son has asked to leave the tribe. He turned the keys to his semi truck over to me this morning. He is moving his family to Florida and going to work for a trucking company there. It is you and I who will chart the future course of the tribe. If anything happens to me, you will be next in line to be chief. Night Shadow's illegitimate child is a girl and not eligible."

"I will do my best to back you in your position as chief, Three Toes. You will make a good one and I will be pleased to have your backside and be your friend. Our two wives to be, however, are not exactly friends."

"They will get over it. Women squabble. I think it comes natural to them. If they were younger, we would give them babies to keep their arms full and their minds off of pettiness."

Gray Feather laughed. " I haven't been with a woman in so long, I am not sure I know how to make a baby. Moon Dance may be getting a dud. "

"I imagine your brain fog won't include forgetting how to sing and howl at the moon." Three Toes laughed slapping him on the back.

"May I ask you how you got the name of three Toes?"

"When I was born, Grandmother Moon Dance was surprised to find that I had three big toes on one foot besides the four regular toes. That is the reason for my wide toed boot. I have seven toes on that foot and three of them are big toes. The extra two big toes have been a real nuisance. I have considered having them removed. If you want to give me clarity on something as a medicine man, explain to me why I am a freak with three big toes?"

"You were one of triplets in your mother's womb. You swallowed or absorbed two of your siblings who were possibly too frail to make it."Gray Feather replied.

"The two extra toes are those of your brothers."

Three Toes laughed. "That is a better explanation than anyone else has ever given me. Hissing Cat is going to get three lovers in one man."

Gray Feather broke out in laughter. "Don't tell Moon Dance. I wouldn't want her to choose you instead of me the dud."

"What do I owe you, Gray Feather?" Three Toes asked laughing about the last remark. I am going out on the truck this afternoon and I could bring you back something that you would like to have instead of throwing a pack of cigarettes in your basket."

"On Christmas Eve, a huge box of individual chocolates was left by one of the town's church groups. The sweets were divided between all the women of the tribe. Would it be possible for you to get me a box in November when the desert cools down so the chocolate won't melt? I would like to surprise Moon Dance. "

"That is not a bad idea, Gray Feather. I will buy a box for Hissing Cat also. We might as well get off on the right foot with our new wives."

After his talk with Three Toes and his realization that he had fallen in love with Moon Dance, Gray Feather made his last evening trip to the tee pee which was Pansy Sky Walker's home. She had lost over two hundred pounds and was now starting to live a fairly normal life weighing somewhere around a hundred and sixty or seventy pounds. Gray Feather had been with the tribe two and one half years and most of that time had believed it was Pansy he was interested in. Now, he was going to have to tell his friend he wouldn't be coming anymore at night to talk or spend time with her. Moon Dance would be his wife and he would be faithful to her. He was Catholic and believed in fidelity.

"Good Evening, Pansy Sky Walker," He stated walking up to her Tee-pee.

Pansy was standing outside leaning against her old rusted green cad waiting for him.

"You are late, Gray Feather. I thought we were going to walk out into the dessert and sit on the lover's dune and disgust the shooting star we saw last night."

"Tonight will be the last night I come to visit with you in the evenings. I have spoken with Three Toes and have chosen a Weelo woman to wed when he becomes chief. Our choices will be announced the night he accepts his position. I cannot see you anymore, Pansy, except in group situations."

"You have got to be kidding. You were on the sand dune with me last night with your arm around me. You can forget marrying anyone but me. I will go to

Three Toes about it. You owe me. I found you in the desert and I have the right to claim you for a husband. What are you, another Night Shadow sneaking around behind my back eyeing and sleeping with someone else? When I get my hands on whatever Weelo woman you have traded me in for, there won't be enough of her left to love."

"I once thought I was in love with you, Pansy. However, I can now see I needed you because I had nothing to cling to. Time has let me come to grips with my memory loss and I am functioning now. I didn't expect my heart to run for someone other than you, but it has. I have already spoken with Three Toes and he has agreed to the woman I will take to my bed."

"Who is she?" Pansy asked with fire in her eyes expecting him to name one of the younger skinnier women in the tribe.

"I am a medicine man, a man of respect. Three Feathers and I both will proclaim our choices on the night he accepts the position of chief. Till then, it is a secret between me, Three Toes, and the Great Spirit."

"I won't let this happen, Gray Feather. I will stand up at the counsel fire and put a stop to your marrying whoever you have chosen stating I own you because I found you. You will marry me and no one else."

"In my mind, I am already married to the woman I have chosen. Our hearts run hand in hand across the night sky as I sleep next to her. I won't be coming to visit in the evenings after tonight. I will be faithful to the other half of my heart."

"I own you Gray Feather. I saved you when you were dying in the middle of a street."

"Grandmother Moon Dance owns me, not you. She saved my life and nursed me back to health, not you. My choice will be okay with her."

CHAPTER ELEVEN

BOOTS OUTSIDE THE DOOR

S ummer passed and the tribe moved into fall with its routine of hunting and storing what they could for the winter months. Gray Feather continued his work as the male tribe medicine man curing thoughts and occasionally helping someone with a health issue. His brain fog was permanent with only an occasional thirty second flash of events that never seemed to make sense. Most of them were of animals in cages and of a big yellow dog with brown eyes. Two names occasionally popped into his mind but not a face to go with them. The names, Carol and Archer, were white men's names. This always made him wonder if he wasn't possibly married to a white woman named Carol Archer that he couldn't remember. However, he couldn't remember anything about the dog or its name. It was just a big yellow dog that was following him around.

Five months or so had passed by and Grandmother Moon Dance still hadn't set Night Shadow's boots outside the door. He continued to disrespect her and chase the younger women of the tribe. Gray Feather continued to sleep on his blanket beneath the kitchen window wishing that the first cold spell at night would arrive so he could return to Moon Dance's Bed. He had resigned himself to the fact that he was in love with a woman that was three times his age and that he was in a time warp waiting for her to make the decision to stay with or divorce the grandfather. She did not know that Gray Feather was in love with her or intended to marry her. He was just patiently waiting for the next twist and turn on his wheel of life as a Weelo Indian medicine man.

Storage was a problem in the Weelo tribe, especially during the Christmas Season when the charities from town delivered baskets of food and boxes of used clothing for the poor Indians. Grandmother Moon Dance's Hogan was the designated area for receiving and storage. In the winter after Christmas, it wasn't unusual for the Grandmother to be sleeping on top of a row of cardboard cases of canned goods for a couple of months till the food supply dwindled down. It was Christmas Eve and the yearly charity madness was starting. Three Toes would be arriving home later with supplies for the hunting season and Gray Feather's box of chocolates for Moon Dance. Coveted amongst the items stored in the Hogan were boxes of old news magazines. There were no televisions or radios in the camp because there was no electricity. Magazines, no matter how old they were, were saved and distributed in the month of January with each family getting one or two. Each day, the families would turn over their share of the magazines to the family in the camp on their right till all of the magazines had been rotated and read by everyone in the tribe. A box of these was stored on the bottom shelf of Moon Dance's kitchen cabinet. They weren't disturbed till the first day of January when the tribe needed entertainment to pass away January and February days. Gray Feather decided that was the perfect place to hide his box of chocolates for moon Dance till he was ready to give them to her. He would hide them later in the day when Three Toes delivered them to him beneath the stack of magazines in the box.

Gray Feather went about his business for the morning counseling the tribe. Grandmother Moon Dance with the help of two women from the tribe graciously accepted what visitors to the camp delivered. Some were charity handouts. Some were gifts from Churches and other types of organizations. Christmas Eve in the Weelo camp wasn't about decorated Christmas trees or wrapped gifts. It was about storing items for survival for the next three months. Every item, no matter what, was accepted graciously; even boxes of magazines or used clothing. The women braided sitting rugs out of used clothing given them.

About noon, the influx of cars let up and Grandmother Moon Dance took a seat on Gray Feather's sitter rug. He was surprised seeing her do so. She had came to him and asked for advice only once or twice in the three years since his brain fog. She was all knowledge in the Weelo camp and rarely was there a question that she couldn't answer.

"What question do you have for the Great Spirit on this White man's Christmas Eve?" he asked in his most professional medicine man voice.

"I love someone dearly that I must leave behind when the Great Mother Ship comes for me. I want to know if I am making the right decision. I have always put the needs of the true blood ancient Weelo ones first. I did not expect to fall in love with a human and believe his heart is the other half of mine. I don't see how this can be. I am not human. How can half of my heart in him be human?"

"Is this why you have not set the boots of Grandfather Night Shadow out the door? Is he the human heart that you cannot let go? I have seen and know how he disrespects you as a woman. I don't have to ask the Great Spirit about that. I know it from living under your Hogan roof for the last three years."

"The running of the heart is unpredictable, Gray Feather." She replied not answering the question about the boots and avoiding telling who her heart raced for."

"Has Three Toes spoken with you about Night Shadow?" He asked feeling his way around her need for counseling.

"Yes, Three Toes has spoken with me. I have cried rivers of tears when no one has been looking. The grandfather and I have spent over fifty years of life together, him as a human and me as an incarnate. I mated with him to produce bodies for the true Weelo to incarnate in. We had ancient ones about to cease needing new bodies. Four of our ancient ones have perished in bodies produced by me. Night Shadow, being human with addictions, taught our four oldest sons who were ancient ones to drink and drive. A car wreck took their lives. My other two children are human like Night Shadow and see me as a crazy old woman who waits for a great fabled ship to come. They disrespect me just like their father who does not see me as I am. I am not crazy, Gray Feather. I am old, tired, and need a new body to enter. Our tribe has quit reproducing. Only two children have born to the Weelo tribe in the last seventeen years. I may cease to be before there is a body available for me. My only hope is for the Great Mother ship to come so I can board."

"The spirit in you, Moon Dance, has the ability to make your body live. People are ill and grow old because they think themselves so. Thinking is the fountain of youth. You must think yourself young and discard that which tries to make you feel old, ugly, and less than you are. If you are an ancient one as you have indicated, then it is your duty to the pure Weelo to live and wait for the mother ship no matter what. Unless a man supports you with his words and efforts, you should discard him as unnecessary to your survival. Light and dark cannot walk together. Honor and disrespect cannot live and walk together. You must decide what is best for you as an ancient one as well as what is best for those in the tribe who are ancient ones incarnated. Good choices are always honored by the Great Spirit even though they may break our heart in making them. If I felt I was the head of an ancient tribe of beings that are not human, I would make whatever decision necessary to ensure their survival, even if it meant the silencing of my running heart for someone. Do my words give you clarity?"

"I resigned myself when young to put up with Night Shadow in his humanness to bear much needed bodies for the ancient ones to incarnate in. I see now thru your words it is time to throw Night Shadow out like the garbage he has become. I will regroup the pure Weelo. I am confident that the Great Mother Ship is coming in less than ten years. Till then, we may need to step into the white men's conceptions to survive. I will lay down the running of my heart like a deer. It is not necessary and I am past the age in this body of bearing children. I must make all decisions with what is best for the ancient ones as the number one priority. I will not let love or the lack of it rule my decisions."

"You won't stop loving me, will you?"

"I will love you till the Great Mother Ship comes for me. After that, I cannot promise you."

"Till death do us part or till the Great Mother ship comes is all that anyone is promised, Moon Dance. I want to lie in your arms and in your bed till that time comes. Three Toes has agreed to let me marry you, should you set Night Shadow's boots outside the door. Three Toes plans to marry Hissing Cat."

"Thank you for the respect, Gray Feather. Come to my bed tonight. You may warm your cold feet on my back side till the Great Mother Ship comes. However, I cannot take you aboard the Great Mother Ship with me. I must take Pansy Sky Walker who is the walking history book of our life on this planet. I am only allowed to bring one human on board with me."

Gray Feather reached over and hugged Moon Dance's shoulders and kissed her on the side of the face. It would be a great honor tonight for me to become Mr. Gray Feather Moon Dance!"

Grandmother Moon Dance looked over at him and grinned with a sudden sparkle in her eyes. "You would take my name like the white women take the name of the white men when they marry?"

"You are a greater medicine man than me. I will be the foot warmer and you can wear the pants in our family. I am okay with that. As a man and Weelo, I know what a treasure you are." He leaned his head over against hers and held her tightly for a moment.

"I may need to leave suddenly some night with the ancient ones in tow should we need white birth conceptions to step into. Will you go with me no questions asked?"

"Where ever you go, Moon Dance, I will go no questions asked. You have owned me for three years. It has been a wonderful time and I have enjoyed every moment with you. Without you, I don't have a life. You are my life and where ever you go, I go."

"That is the answer that I am looking for. Thank you, Gray Feather. Come to my bed tonight and I will warm my cold feet on you. Just so you know, only about a dozen of the ancient ones have survived. They are Howling Wolf, Walks Crooked, Three Toes, Hissing Cat, Running Deer, North Star, and a missing one of us who accidentally entered a body named Benson and lives in the East and works as a mind doctor. Benson will find his way home to us before the Great Mother Ship arrives. A few of us were washed away in the Great Flood without homing chips. We have no way of knowing whether they have survived or been able to step down thru the centuries from body to body. It is possible that there might be a few Weelo on far distant shores.

"The name Benson sounds really familiar to me, like he is lost somewhere in my brain fog. I am sure that I know him. Isn't that strange?" he asked wondering about the image he was seeing of a man with a shelf full of books and Indian statuary. The memory was just a brief flash.

"Everything we do as Weelo is strange because we are not human. We are Weelo existing in human bodies. Right now, I need a new one. The one you see is wearing out. However, I would like to wear it out loving you. I can see myself with a big belly and you the cause."

"You would be willing to have a happy accident with me?" He asked grinning from ear to ear.

"The white women speak of happy accidents. Benson was a happy accident to his white human parents who were traveling thru our dessert as tourists. Their car broke down after dark and they spent the night sleeping on a blanket on the dessert sand. The human woman conceived not knowing that she was within a quarter of a mile from our camp. One of our ancient ones thought she was a producer of bodies for the Weelo. Benson entered the tourist woman's body and into the baby's form that a human soul had not entered yet. He was a happy accident and his human parents have raised him well on the East coast. We are able to communicate with him thru dreams. Our great regret was the loss of our great scientist and doctor, Captain Noah Archer. We don't know if he is alive or ceased to be. We have always assumed he lost his life drowning in the Great Flood. North Star, who has is our vision communicator, keeps seeing him in the bottom of a bottle somewhere. She says he will make his way to us."

"You and I have found each other. Will tonight be a time of a possible happy accident? "Gray Feather asked grinning from ear to ear and trying to stir the conversation back to babies."

"I don't know, Gray Feather. However, I am sure we will find much pleasure trying." She retorted grinning equally as big."

"Would there be any chance of us trying before tonight?" he asked ribbing her and eyeing the sparkle in her eyes. The sparkle in her eyes was what got to him.

"When Night Shadow's boots are out the door, come inside and we will try for a happy accident. I think I am willing to before nighttime."

"How quick can you set his boots out?"

"If you will let go of my shoulders, I believe I could get the mission accomplished in the next five minutes and then sing the white man's Christmas song of here comes Santa Claus."

Gray feather released her shoulders. "Let me help you up," he replied laughing and then went to singing here comes Santa Claus as she left his sitter rug. Too his dismay, he had two tribal members waiting for counsel. That was just his luck.

Grandmother Moon Dance giggled and left his side whistling.

CHAPTER TWELVE

MICHAEL'S REMAINS

It was Christmas Eve morning and Doctor Ralph Archer had just finished delivering a batch of high risk puppies, an emergency. He was speaking with the pet's owner when his conversation was interrupted by his nurse sticking her head in the door. Even though it was a holiday, they were staying open until noon. Animals were like humans. They ate holiday goodies they shouldn't have and got equally as ill. His waiting room was full of animals needing something. Recently he had hired an assistant and it was taking them both to wade thru the Christmas Eve morning madness.

"Dr. Archer, there are two gentleman dressed in black out here to speak with you. They say it is concerning Dr. Haven. I think they have found an item belonging to him. They are carrying a brown envelope marked evidence on the side."

Ralph's color drained from his face and he was instantly a bundle of nerves. He had waited for three years for some news concerning his friend's disappearance. The private investigator, he had hired in Texas, had come up with nothing. Michael had just disappeared into nowhere. In the back of his mind, he had killed his friend by inviting him to be his best man. To cope the last three years, he had become an alcoholic and had spent several stays in a private psych hospital drying out.

His hands were trembling. The agents wouldn't waste their time on Christmas Eve if there was not a reason. Now, they were waiting for him in his waiting room with an evidence box. He excused himself from the pet owner and headed quickly for the front area of the clinic. He wasn't sure he could handle it if they finally said Michael was dead. However, he knew that had to be the case. There had not been any activity on Michael's credit cards or bank accounts since the day of the wedding on Christmas Eve three years prior.

Ralph Archer took a deep breath and exhaled as he walked to the lobby. He wanted a drink bad to calm his nerves. Michael was like a brother to him. He had been totally distraught at not knowing what had happened to him after they ran from the chapel in Bullhorn, Texas where he had dumped his bride to be. He wished now that he had gone ahead and married Connie. His friend would be alive.

Entering the lobby, he greeted the two men in black whom he knew were FBI agents.

"I am Dr. Archer. My nurse said you wish to speak with me about Dr. Haven."

"We better step into your office to discuss what we have come about. I am agent Carl Craig."

"Of course . . . follow me," Ralph stated leading the way to his office and then closing the door behind the two men once they were inside. "Have you found Michael or have a clue of some sort? My private detective in Texas has come up with nothing."

"An archaeologist on a dig last month in the New Mexico dessert came across an item that we think is the robe that your friend was wearing the day he disappeared. We want you to look at a picture of it."Agent Craig stated removing a photo from the brown envelope.

Ralph, with hands suddenly perspiring, took the photo held out to him by the agent. In shock, he immediately sat down in his office swivel desk chair and burst into tears. "You took my robe years ago as possible evidence. This is Michaels except that the wings are missing and it looks like a tattered rag."

"Dr. Archer, the wings are missing as you have indicated. They were probably chewed off and eaten by wild animals in the dessert. Three years in the dessert has taken its toll on the garment. It is too far gone to obtain any type of DNA or other evidence from it. The Archaeologist took us to where he found it. However, the robe could have been dragged by animals or blown by the wind miles from where it was discarded. Your friend could not have walked out of the dessert from where the robe was found. Your friend was barefoot on the day he disappeared. I want to remind you that his billfold, shoes, etc. were in the back of that rental van. Barefoot and without water he could not have survived in the dessert. It is our opinion that someone abducted your friend within three blocks of the church, discarded his clothing, and then took him into the New Mexico dessert and left him there barefoot and in that robe to die. We are also sure that you were the intended target by you know who but we cannot prove it."

Tears rolling down his face, Ralph stated. "Michael was an animal activist. He never let a dog or cat go for a moment without water here or at his home. The thought of him dying from heat and thirst is appalling."

"I am sorry, Dr. Archer. Your friend in our opinion is dead and his bones are somewhere in the vast wastelands of New Mexico. It is just a fluke that the Archaeologist found the robe. As we told you on the phone a couple years back, the driver of the rental van that was working on a fishing boat as a cook was not your friend. He stated he was only parked along that curb in Texas for about fifteen minutes, just long enough to pick up a few things from a friend that he was taking to Oregon with him. There was a fifteen minute time frame and that was when his possessions were thrown or placed into the back of the truck. Someone took your friend, discarded his possessions, and then transported him to the wastelands of New Mexico and apparently left him there."

"So, you are confident that Michael is dead?" Ralph asked with red tear filled eyes.

"We have no body, Dr. Archer. However, we have this robe and it was the last clothing he was seen wearing. There has been no activity on his credit cards, bank accounts, social security number, or telephone calls made to anyone he knew including the kennel owner where he left his dog. Yes, we feel he is dead and the chance of us finding his bones in that vast wasteland is not good."

"Will you send my nurse in on your way out? I don't want my pet owners to see me like this." He said with tears rolling and his hands trembling.

"We are sorry, Dr. Archer. Unless bones or some other evidence shows up, the case now goes into our cold files."

"Thank you for coming and telling me. I am never going to be able to forgive myself for this. He saved me from marrying Connie Carlson and then lost his life for it."

"I would suggest you get some counseling, Dr. Archer. You are just as much of a victim as your friend. Do it for him. Drinking isn't going to make the event go away. We know how many times you have been picked up the last three years for drinking and driving? We have kept track of you. You drink, drive, get picked up and ramble on and on how your friend saved your ass and then lost his. It is time to hold a funeral for your friend, lay him to rest, and go on with your life."

After the agents left, Ralph called Jennifer, Michael's former girlfriend. They had bonded in the months after Michael disappeared. Six months after Michael's disappearance, they married one night when both of them were drunk. The marriage was not intentional for either of them. They now had two children, a two year old boy and a newborn baby girl. He rang his home phone and she answered.

Jo Hammers

"Jennifer, FBI agents have just left my office. They found the robe that Michael was wearing the day he disappeared. He is dead, eaten by wild animals in the back waste lands of New Mexico. The robe is all that is left of him." Ralph Archer stated and then burst into uncontrollable sobbing and hung up the phone. Leaving his office, he exited the back door of his veterinarian clinic and headed for the nearest liquor store. There he purchased and fell into a bottle of vodka and didn't climb back out for three weeks.

CHAPTER THIRTEEN

A COLD WIND BLOWS

Acold wind started to blow and Gray Feather was pleased as he prepared to read for his last two Christmas Eve Sitters. He glanced over to the Hogan Door and saw that the Grandmother had set Night Shadow's boots out. He was really pleased and couldn't wait for the charity women to quit coming, night to fall, and the Weelo women helping Moon Dance to go home to their families. He hadn't been with a woman since before his brain fog and he was more than ready. He was excited and ready to howl like a wolf. He was glad he waited. Moon Dance was the one, the other half of his heart.

As he was sitting on his rug counseling Road Runner, he saw one of the women leave the Hogan with a shocked expression on her face and holding a magazine tight to her bosom as though she were hiding the cover. She didn't speak to Gray Feather, but headed quickly to the bullet shaped travel trailer of Three Toes, knocked, and entered closing the door. Three Toes had pulled his semi in about thirty minutes prior. He had been out on a long haul. Gray Feather wondered what it was all about, but he didn't have time to get up and inquire of Moon Dance or Three Toes. He was sure that Moon Dance would tell him about it later, whatever the problem was. However, he was more interested in making love to Moon Dance than tackling a tribe problem.

As he sat there, Grandmother Moon Dance suddenly exited the Hogan with a really strange look on her face not smiling and also headed for the silver bullet shaped travel trailer of Three Toes. "The women must all be in to it again." he muttered to himself.

Cat fights were common amongst the Weelo women. He watched as the first woman exited Three Toes' trailer, went and got her husband, and once more entered Three Toes' Trailer. Moon Dance did not come out. The husband came out and went and knocked on two trailer doors whispering to the men who immediately followed the first husband to the trailer. This went on till every male in the place, except Gray Feather, had visited Three Toes Trailer. The male who was waiting to see Gray Feather, seeing something was up, left and also went to Three Toes trailer. Counseling sessions over, Gray Feather sat and watched the crowd gathered at the future chief's trailer with curiosity. However, he didn't want to get involved because he had plans for him and Moon Dance later. He wasn't going to get caught up mediating some cat fight or tribal matter that could go on all night. So, he sat still and waited for Moon Dance to return. It was getting cold, so he covered up with the sitter rug which was not occupied.

In about thirty minutes or so, Three Toes exited his trailer and headed toward Gray Feather.

"Oh crap . . ." muttered Gray Feather. "They are going to force me to participate in whatever the craziness is. Damn it."

Three Toes pointed to the ground and Gray Feather took the sitter rug and spread it for Three Toes to sit on. He immediately sat down, crossed his legs, and was visibly shaken. He pulled a pack of cigarettes from his pocket, tapped the pack on his leg, and immediately lit one and took a drag.

"I gather something is up. Do you want to tell me what the problem is?" asked Gray Feather abandoning his usual introductory line of 'What would you ask of the Great Spirit'.

"I am here on behalf of Moon Dance and this is difficult for me to have to say considering the discussion we had in July concerning her. I don't know how to approach you about this and hope you won't hold it against me personally."

"Has Hissing Cat and Moon Dance been at odds today over something?"

Three Toes bit his lip and then took another drag off of his cigarette. "Moon Dance has changed her mind and wishes you to move out of her Hogan as well as Night Shadow. She thinks she made a mistake in her conversations with you today and she wishes to take all of her words back. She wants me to tell you that she is releasing her ownership of you and you may go live with Pansy Sky Walker. She says to tell you that she will remain single and not marry at all. She will wait for the Great Mother Ship and enter alone."

"What . . .? She invited me to her bed not more than three hours ago. What have I done?" Gray Feather asked in shock.

"You have not done anything. It is the Grandmother's decision. I have come to escort you to Pansy's tee pee the only available lodging in the village. The tribe has agreed that is where you belong. A one by one vote of the men has taken place. Moon Dance will stay in my trailer till you get your things. Starting tomorrow, you will counsel outside Pansy Sky Walker's tee pee door.

"You have got to let me talk to Moon Dance. I love her, Three Toes."

"The tribe has voted and spoken. You now belong to Pansy Sky Walker. She found you in the dessert and you no longer need the medical care of Moon Dance."

"I want a reason why she is kicking me out." he demanded with his face suddenly flushed.

"Grandmother Moon Dance needs no reason. She is Weelo. A Weelo woman can divorce a man just by putting his boots outside the door. You are not married to her, so all she needs do is find you somewhere to go. That she has done. She came to my trailer and the task has been accomplished. You will sleep at Pansy Sky Walker's dwelling."

Gray Feather rose to his feet. Six of the Weelo men had come to assist Three Toes in case there was a problem. They all knew that Gray Feather had lived in the lodge for three years and expected to marry Moon Dance.

Reluctantly, Gray Feather gathered up his two little rugs and his sleeping rug from the inside of the Hogan and left the only home he knew with tears in his eyes. The men escorted him to Pansy Sky Walker's Tee Pee. He threw what little he owned into the back of Pansy's old rusted, green cad with no intentions of going inside. He was pissed and when the men were gone, he headed for the lover's dune where he could be alone and try to figure out what had happened that she would change her mind about him. He was hurt, mad, and pissed to his core.

Gray Feather didn't know that the Weelo woman, who had left the Hogan holding a magazine to her bosom, had discovered his photo on the front cover his photo and inside an article about his possible kidnapping and disappearance from a Texas wedding. In shock, she had also read about the involvement of Pete Carlson who was Pansy Sky Walker's father. The FBI was looking for Gray Feather who was not a medicine man but a missing doctor from New Jersey. Pansy Sky Walker had kidnapped him and brought trouble to the tribe's door. The tribe had made a quick decision and delivered what they considered to be trouble back to Pansy's door. All the charity groups had seen Gray Feather as they delivered baskets of food and various items to the Hogan, including the box of outdated news magazines. If their tribal member recognized him from the magazine cover photo, it was possible one of the town's charity women might have done the same. The tribe was innocent as was their medicine woman, Grandmother Moon Dance. The quick general consensus was that the tribe needed to move the camp secretly leaving no trace that they ever existed. They could not afford for their identity to be discovered. They had waited for thousands of years for the Great Mother ship to come for them and they were just one to seven years from it happening. Now was not the time to go to war with the United States or the country

Jo Hammers

to go to war with them.

Christmas Eve passed with a guard posted at the Hogan door to prevent Gray Feather from returning there. Gray Feather spent a lonely Christmas Eve staring at what was his home and realizing all of his memories existed there. He would give Moon Dance a little time and then go to her. She couldn't have stopped loving him. He had always put her first and her needs ahead of his own. He loved her. He wondered if perhaps she might have had a minor brain fart, a small stroke that might have caused her to reject him. His own brain fart had been major.

Gray Feather slept cold in the back seat of Pansy Sky Walker's old green cad covering himself with his sleeping rug. He wasn't used to sleeping out in the open and in the night air. He awoke with a runny nose. Spending Christmas Eve in the back seat of a dirty old car was not what he had planned. He had planned to make love to her and establish a relationship with her. Fate had delivered to him cold feet and a nose that was dripping. Pansy Sky Walker's old, rusted, green cad convertible's cloth top had worn out and blew away years ago. Pansy wasn't home, so he didn't dare sleep in her Tee-pee without permission. He had just told her that he planned to marry someone other than her. She was not going to be overly friendly.

Pansy had caught a bus to Texas for Christmas. Being half white, she celebrated the white man's holiday. She never stayed around the camp to help with the Christmas storage and the sorting of Christmas baskets delivered. She wanted to be white and stalked her father and sister incessantly.

Wiping his nose on the back of his hand, he decided he was going to have to rough it till she got back. He wasn't happy about it and he was going to have to eat his words about loving someone else. Pansy was not going to let him live it down, especially when she learned he had chosen Grandmother Moon Dance.

Gray Feather had spent a miserable night and had questioned himself as to what he did to get himself thrown out. He loved Moon Dance. He also asked himself why he even existed. In his brain fog, all he had was his memories with her. She was his whole world and now that world had collapsed around him. He was nothing without her. He would go see Moon Dance after she cooled down. He deserved to know why she had thrown him out. He had always been there for her.

It was early morning on Christmas Day. Gray Feather was scrounging around for some cookies in Pansy's old car and found a few stale ones in the glove compartment. The old green cad hadn't been in running condition for over a year. It wasn't going to be much of a home, but it looked like it was his new home. He was really pissed as he thought about the hot mush and cornbread he ate in the

106

Hogan every morning. Cookies were a poor substitute. He had moved from Heaven to Hell in his opinion.

As he was eating the stale cookies, Hissing Cat approached him walking very slowly across the center common ground with one of the younger women of the tribe assisting her. Gray Feather tried to smooth his braid. Moon Dance always braided his hair first thing in the morning. He was sure he looked a mess having slept in his clothes. He was also unshaven. Moon Dance always seemed amused when he shaved in the morning. None of the tribe had facial hair except him. Three Toes kept him in razors, buying them out on the road.

"Good morning, Gray Feather," Hissing Cat stated as she reached the old cad and stood leaning on it.

"Good morning, Hissing Cat. May I ask the nature of your early morning visit?"

"I would like to say that I am here to entice you into calling on me, now that Moon Dance doesn't want you. However, I have barely shuffled my way here to speak with you concerning the women of the tribe. Are your feet cold this morning?" She asked grinning from ear to ear. She was over ninety.

"I am single, if that is what you are asking. My feet are indeed cold and I am pissed. I don't know why Moon Dance threw me out." He replied not grinning. "If I had it to do over, I would pursue you. At least I could catch you and keep you in my arms. Moon Dance has run from me."

"Being old and walking slow has its advantages. You may chase and catch me if you choose. My body may be old, but my spirit knows a good looking man when I see it. Moon Dance is a fool." She replied."Come to my trailer at noon and I will have you something hot fixed to eat."

"The long cold night and these stale cookies for breakfast are killing my love for Moon Dance. You, however, are growing in my heart." He replied laughing."I like a woman that can cook. Shuffling isn't a problem with me."

"I can see that your nose is starting to run and that you will need someone to care for you. I am willing. You may sleep on my trailer floor tonight. Perhaps, Moon Dance will come to her senses when she sees you in the lodge trailer of a chief's wife." She stated winking at him.

"Not only will I sleep and eat at your place. I will bring you chocolates." He stated thinking that Moon Dance would be green with envy knowing he was giving her chocolates."

"Bring the chocolate and yourself. Counsel the women and accept whatever propositions you want. You are single and it is okay with me. Take a break mid-morning and I will braid your hair and put a chief's feather in it. That will really piss off Moon Dance."

"Thank you, Hissing Cat. I won't forget this."

"She does not know what she has discarded. I do. You are pure Weelo and have made your way home to us. I know a chief when I see one. If I were guessing, you are one our ancient ones that got washed away in the Great Flood. We had a great scientist on board named Doctor Havenio. In my thinking you are him. He did not eat meat. Your brain fog is preventing you from remembering. In ancient times, your hair was golden and your skin was golden like the beams of the Weelo sun."

"I am glad you see me as special. I don't have a clue as to who I am except for three years I have loved and made memories with Moon Dance. Maybe I need to sit at your feet and make new memories. I like your story about the Great Scientist named Havenio with golden hair and skin."

Hissing cat turned and shuffled back across the dessert to her travel trailer.

Sitting down on his rug in front of Pansy Sky Walker's Tee Pee, he prepared to counsel the long line of women that was forming. What he didn't know was that the women were told by the husbands and men of the tribe to go for counsel to give the men a chance to meet out in the desert and decide what to do about Pansy's kidnapping of the New Jersey doctor they knew as Gray Feather. They were told to keep him busy with each taking a twenty minute turn on the rug to give them a chance to discuss and vote on Pansy's and Gray Feather's fate. They weren't sure whether just leaving them behind would solve their problem.

It was Christmas Day and the Weelo men, one by one, grabbed a rifle and walked off into the desert as though they were going hunting. They were having a tribal meeting three miles out into the dessert where no one back at camp could hear what would probably be some heated discussions. All the men went including any boy over the age of four who was able to walk that far. Eleven year old Howling Wolf, with his BB gun over his shoulder, joined the line of men walking into the desert. He was told to be the last in line and was appointed lookout to make sure that Gray Feather didn't follow. He took his appointed position seriously and walked backwards part of the time guarding the rear.

Gray Feather watched the men walk off into the dessert with their guns. He never went hunting because he was opposed to killing animals. However, he ate meat when there was nothing else to eat. Hunger will make you eat anything. He had found that out.

Running Deer was the first woman in line. He smiled and motioned for her to sit on his sitter's rug. She had pulled her semi truck in late the night before. He was surprised that she was up so early and first in line. She probably hadn't had three or four hours of sleep. Running Deer was about the age of Three Toes. She was in her early forties and was always seen dressed in jeans, driver's boots, and a T-shirt like a man. On her fingers were multiple turquoise rings. Her ears hosted long dangly beaded and feathered earrings. After seating herself, she removed her heavy cumbersome driving boots before crossing her legs which was the custom for seeing and speaking with a medicine man. Her toenails were painted a bright red when she pulled her naked feet out of the boots. She took a deep breath and then turned to look at the medicine man and handed him a note to read.

Gray Feather opened the note and read her scribble.

Don't say anything. Something is wrong in the camp . The men are in the desert voting and the women have been told to keep you busy. You are in serious trouble. I got in late and don't know what for. The women woke me up and told me to get in line. Counsel me on the clap or something saying this is lab results.

Gray Feather turned and stared into Running Deer's eyes seeing a friend that he didn't know he had.

"These lab results are shocking, Running Deer. I do agree that you are going to have to take several rounds of antibiotics to overcome your catching of the white man's virus of the hissing snake." He stated loudly for the line to hear. He heard a long line of whispers and giggles ensuing."

Running Deer grinned at him and reached over and patted him on the knee and then ran her hand up his leg in a seductive fashion. He let her knowing she was covering her traitor to the tribe ass. She considered herself to be a modern Weelo woman who saw no need to have a husband. She openly slept with who- ever she wanted Weelo or white.

"I slept with the wrong white buck and now I have the yellow muck." She stated loudly taking out a pack of miniature cigars and lighting one. "Should I refrain from sharing it with the four or five tribe husbands who want to make me their number two wife?"

A hush fell over the line of women who were waiting. Each woman there lis- tened in hopes of hearing some good adultery gossip.

"That won't be necessary," he replied. "I can cure you. I will come to your truck mid morning and bring a medicine bag."

"Thank you, Gray Feather. I will wait for you and sleep with you in payment for your services, if you are willing." She stated loud enough for the line to hear and run taking the words to Grandmother Moon Dance.

"I accept your payment, Running Deer." He stated loudly hoping Moon Dance was somewhere near listening. Maybe he needed to make her jealous to get back in her good graces."

Running Deer rose and turned over the sitter's rug to the next woman in line. Gray Feather alarmed wadded the note up and put it in his worn out jean's pocket.

Fifth in line was a very young tribe wife named North Star. She was sixteen or seventeen and very tiny. She took her position on the sitter's rug with a red face and waited for the medicine man to speak to her.

"What would you ask of the Great Spirit this morning?" he asked trying to remain calm and not let the women know that he knew they were purposely choosing long explanation questions to keep him busy.

"I am a young wife and I do not understand everything there is to know about conception and sex positions. May I whisper my question in your ear? I am really embarrassed about having to inquire of you about it." She asked looking him in the eye with pleading eyes.

"Yes, whisper in my ear and I will whisper the answer back to you," he stated grinning at her.

"You have got to take Pansy and run. She has brought trouble to the camp and the men are thinking of doing away with her. You are the trouble. You are not one of us and may be dead tomorrow. I haven't forgotten that you helped me to convince the tribe that I wasn't lying about grandfather Night Shadow molesting me."

Gray Feather put his arm around her and then whispered in her ear. "Do you know why I am trouble? Blush if you can and pretend to ask me another question." He released his arm from around her.

"I am to lie on my back with my feet high in the air and do what . . .?" she yelled slapping her hand over her mouth.

Gray Feather grinned. She was quite a little actress and he was discovering that he had friends that he didn't realize were watching out for him. He was also learning which women of the tribe were not his friends by their idle questions and chatter. He leaned his ear in to North Star so she could continue.

"A box of magazines in Moon Dance's Hogan holds the answer. I must rise or they may think there is something between you and I."

"I understand," he whispered back and she immediately rose from her position on the rug and walked to the nearest young wife her age and said loudly, "You won't believe what he told me. I will be pregnant by tomorrow if I can get my husband in from the dessert to do his duty."

All the women in the line giggled and laughed intending to ask her privately sometime soon concerning what mystical thing he had told her. There was a shortage of babies in the tribe. Walking Crooked was the last birth and she was five going on six now.

Mid morning, Gray Feather rose stating he needed to relieve himself and take a short nap due to his brain fog that occasionally produced a headache. He told the women to return in forty-five minutes and he would continue. He commonly took a mid day nap, so they thought nothing about it. Then he told them he also needed to take Running Deer a medicine bag and that he would be taking his nap on her bunk. The women all smiled ear to ear and broke out in snickers. One spoke loudly saying, "Moon Dance is going to have your hide if she is watching. She and Running Deer are not fond of each other."

"I am a single man. Moon Dance has set me out her door like I am pair of boots. "Running deer owes me payment and I intend to collect."

The women were satisfied with his need to collect payment and went their way. They had all put something in his basket. One of them had put in a box of tissues for his runny nose. Another had put in a small package of cough drops and another put in a bottle of aspirin. It was evident to all of them that he was taking a New Mexico desert cold.

Gray Feather rose and headed for Running Deer's truck. He whistled as he went hoping that Moon Dance heard him. He was pissed and hoped she saw him heading for Running Deer's motel room on wheels.

CHAPTER FOURTEEN

THE DECISION

Three miles away and out of listening distance of the Weelo tribe camp, the men gathered and sat down on the desert sand and talked amongst themselves. The subject was the kidnapping of Doctor Michael Haven and Pansy being the kidnapper. Quick decisions concerning the pair had to be made. The tribe was sure that one of the charity ladies from the day before may have recognized their medicine man as the missing doctor. They were also wondering if Gray Feather's brain fog was just an easy way for him to hide out with them if he had pulled something illegal. In their mind, a rich doctor from New Jersey would not live in poverty with them unless he was running from something.

Three Toes rose to lead the men's tribal meeting of the Weelo. There was only one subject to be discussed. Pansy Sky Walker had brought a stranger into their midst and passed him off as one of them as well as a medicine man. They were sure Gray Feather was innocent of anything illegal from reading the magazine article and that Pansy had kidnapped him. Their fear was that if his memories returned he would go straight to law enforcement.

Three Toes opened the discussion.

"You all know why we have gathered. Our carefully guarded identity as a tribe is at risk of being discovered. Pansy Sky Walker, being only half Weelo, has brought trouble to our door willingly and kept us all in the dark concerning it. Her reason has been self-centered. Gray Feather was to marry her sister, Connie Carlson. As a consensus of thought this morning, we feel she took her sister's groom to get even for years of neglect and rejection by her father Pete Carlson. There is no getting around that Pansy Sky Walker is standing behind Dr. Haven in the magazine photo of the church wedding. There is not a doubt amongst us that she kidnapped him and possibly hit him over the head giving him his brain fog. We could all end up in prison for her selfishness. If he were an ordinary man, we could take him into the desert and leave him. However, Hissing Cat feels he is one of us and has been drawn to us with Pansy being the means of getting him here. If he is Weelo, we cannot do away with him. A few of our ancient ones were lost in the great flood and they may have reproduced and come down thru the centuries as a separate tribe. The flood could have washed the missing ancient ones miles from us and they started over just as we did. We have always assumed those ancient ones were drowned. Perhaps Hissing Cat is right and Gray Feather has made his way to us. He has seemed happy with us. Each of you stand and give your opinion as to what you think we should do with Pansy Sky Walker and the doctor. "

"What about Grandfather Night Shadow? He is not here to vote." One of the younger men in the tribe asked.

"Grandfather Night Shadow was banned from the tribe two days ago. His tongue has been silenced so he cannot speak. He is on one of our trucks now being driven to Florida. He cannot read or write so he will not be able to tell them who he is or where he is from. He is now blind folded so that he cannot find his way back to us. Our women are not safe with him around. The white men will not put up with his molestation crap. Moon Dance has set his boots outside her Hogan door and is free to marry. Night Shadow was human, not pure Weelo. One of our men must step up and marry Moon Dance and take her into their trailer for her safety. We will burn the Hogan and with it the doctor's memories."

"I am willing to take Moon Dance and marry her to keep her safe," Ten year old Howling Wolf stated.

The men of the tribe broke out laughing.

"We respect your offer, Howling Wolf, and you have first claim." Three Toes stated grinning from ear to ear. Howling Wolf liked the grandmother's cooking.

"We must decide now what to do about Pansy Sky Walker. Stand one by one and give your opinion as to what we should do with her. We will vote on the suggestions."

The Road Runner stood first.

"Gray Feather, or Doctor Haven as the news magazine has called him, has harmed none of us. If anything he has counseled and helped all of us to the best of his knowledge and ability. However, should his memory return, he will see us as having used him and he will definitely leave us. I feel we should put him on one of our trucks and return him to the land of New Jersey and set him out on a street corner and give him money for a phone call. While he is on the truck for the two or three day journey we should move the camp and our people by night to a new location and new identities. I also feel we should choose a farm land where we can grown the fruits and vegetables we need, as well as beef, pork, and chicken to eat. We cannot continue to be a nomad type tribe much longer.

Howling Wolf stood next.

"I always thought Pansy Sky Walker was a fat cow till Gray Feather explained to me how important she is to us as the walking history of our tribe. I think we should keep Pansy Sky Walker with us for that reason, but hobble her and not allow her to return to the land of Texas anymore. Gray Feather has been a good medicine man. I am sure that he was a good doctor in New Jersey before he came to us. It would not be a good thing to do away with a doctor, especially an animal doctor. We all know how important an animal doctor would be should the Great Ship come and we gather animals again. I saw we keep him to and just make him drink poisoned moonshine each time he has a memory flash to control him. We need him."

The tribe laughed at the sincerity of Howling Wolf's suggestion for the use of Moonshine.

One by one, the men of the tribe got up and gave their opinions.

One by one the tribe then voted on the many suggestions. When the voting was done, Three Toes rose again to speak and set in motion the will of the tribe.

"The Earth's law enforcement will descend on us here once the medicine man remembers who he is. Members of our tribe will possibly be arrested for kidnapping. He is having more memory flashes all of the time. We are innocent of the kidnapping, but law enforcement will not see it that way. Should they try to arrest and take into custody members of our tribe, we will have to declare war on the United States and rescue our members. We are not looking for trouble, nor do we wish to enter a war in which the United States would cease to be. They are no match for us. The land known as the USA has been home to us while we have secretly waited for the Mother ship. We will remember it as home when we have left and return to the planet Weelo. The tribe has voted and we have agreed that we still need to remain a tribe in secret. We will leave after midnight tonight and take up residence in the land of Utah. Gray Feather will be drugged by Hissing Cat and left behind unharmed. Tomorrow, he will think the camp was a bad dream. The Joseph followers have more than one wife. Our women will be divided amongst us males. We will no longer dress like Indians. We will live and dress in the land of Utah like Joseph extremists. If our calculations are correct, the Great Mother Ship will be coming for us sometime between the next three to seven years.'

"What about Pansy?" a male voice questioned.

"We will keep Pansy Sky Walker, the half breed, with us till Walks Crooked is old enough to memorize all of the history that Pansy has in her. Pansy will be hobbled for her disrespect and never allowed to leave the camp for any reason for bringing such grave trouble to our door on purpose. She is a kidnapper. At the time the Great Mother Ship comes for us. Pansy Sky Walker will be left behind in the wastelands of Utah. We will leave it up to the Great Spirit at that point to let her live or die. She will be alone except for whoever else the tribe considers is not worthy of boarding the Great Mother."

"Will we pull our bullets, or will we fly them?" Howling Wolf asked.

Everyone had always wanted to see one of them fly. The fuel packs in them were preserved for the flight to the mother ship. There was not replacement fuel energy packs to be frivolous with. The bullet flyers had been hidden for thousands of years in deserts and caves preserving them. When the great flood hit and the original mother ship went down, they flew the bullets to a high mountain and preserved them there. Preservation had been the number one concern since then. Making them look like bullet shaped travel trailers had been the preservation technique for the last seventy or so years.

"We will pull the bullets. Men, you will have your campers hooked to your pickups and ready to pull out by midnight. If Gray Feather asks, tell him we are pulling all of them into town thru the car wash so we can paint them. He knows we do everything as a tribe and at the same time. He will not question it. Now everyone return to the tribe and act as if nothing were wrong. Everyone fill their trailers with the Christmas food that was delivered to us yesterday. We will need it to survive. Leave nothing behind. By the time Gray Feather wakes up tomorrow morning, nothing of our camp will remain but the ashes of the Hogan. Howling Wolf, it is your job to set the Hogan on fire as the last trailer leaves. You jump in the back of the pickup pulling it. Do not touch Pansy Sky Walker's Tee Pee or her old car. The doctor will need the two to survive. Everyone beware that just one of the Weelo Planetary atomic bombs on board our bullet flyers is capable of wiping out the entire United States, Canada, and Mexico. We caused a great flood once by dropping a bomb off the coast of ancient Eastern lands. We almost perished when the bomb sent huge waves flooding the coast land. Noah 1, our original Great Mother ship was lost due to our own stupidity. Do not activate or play around with the flyer's dash panel. Only our ancient ones are capable of manning the many controls and know which control is the one to switch on to activate and drop the bombs."

CHAPTER FIFTEEN

ROCKING WITH RUNNING DEER

Meanwhile, back at the Weelo camp, Gray Feather made his way to the plain Jane white Semi-truck cab and knocked. Running Deer lived in the semi just as the tribe did in the trailers. He heard her unlock the door and then stood back as she pushed the door open for him to climb up and in. He was surprised to find it was spotless on the inside. On the driver's bunk was a colorful quilt thrown back where she had apparently been asleep.

"All the women are going to be looking so we have got to make this truck rock for about twenty minutes or so to make it appear I am paying you. She pulled some heavy curtains around the side windows and across the dash to block out the view of the camp. "You get on that end of the bed and I will get on the other and we will rock the cab."

"You are one smart cookie, Running Deer." He stated as they started to rock the truck. She was parked in the middle of the camp. He wondered if Moon Dance was watching. It was her that he wanted to make love to.

"Smart enough to be tired of the crap of the men always being in charge and voting on the life and death rights of others. Weelo women here have no say or rights except for Hissing Cat and Moon Dance. This is the United States and the modern age. I don't go along with the archaic male superiority bullshit."

"Running Deer, I honestly don't know what I have done to upset the tribe. I have waited three years to marry Moon Dance. I intended to sleep with her for the first time last night when all Hell broke loose."

"Pansy has used you somehow to bring law enforcement down our necks. It has something to do with a magazine that one of Moon Dance's helpers found. There was whispers and gossip in the line earlier to that effect. The FBI is looking for you concerning the incident, whatever it was. I haven't had a chance to look at the magazine yet. Did you and Pansy steal something or do something illegal before arriving here? Do you really have a brain fog?"

Gray Feather stopped rocking the cab and Running Deer abandoned her rocking rhythm as well.

"My brain fog is real, Running Deer. If Pansy and I pulled something, it is lost in my fog. I do recall her telling me that I and another man may have drank the holy sacrament wine in a church. Would the government be looking for me for that? I haven't been able to go see a priest and confess for it since arriving here. I am sure that I will probably die and go to hell for it?"

Running Deer began to laugh. "That is the worst thing you have ever done?"

"I drank the Great Spirit's wine. You know how Indians are with their private stash of it and cigarettes."

"I think you are safe on the wine drinking bit, Gray Feather. It is something far more serious. Have you seen Pansy with stolen items or heard her speak of pulling a con of some sort? I heard one of the women telling another in the line that you are on the missing persons TV show and law men are looking for you."

"I don't recall doing anything illegal. Was I a thief and procured things for the reservation before my brain fog?"

"You weren't one of us before your brain fog. Pansy brought you here. She led us to believe she had picked you up hitch hiking and that you were one of the North tribe making your way here to practice medicine. Whatever Pansy has pulled is serious enough that they are considering doing away with her and leaving you in the desert to rot. That is what the women are whispering to each other."

"Oh shit, North Star was telling me the truth."

"The box of magazines stored in the Hogan holds the answers, Gray Feather. Most of the tribe doesn't read. One member of the family usually reads the magazine to the others. Hissing Cat has only seen the cover and there is only one copy floating around amongst the families to read."

"Why would a simple Indian man like me be wanted for?"

"The answer is in the box. I will go pick a cat fight with someone. When the women all have their attention turned on me, you climb down and hurry to the Hogan. Pull the box of magazines and throw them up here into the semi. I have Pansy's welfare to consider as well as yours."

"You think Moon Dance has turned on me because she thinks I might be Pansy's partner in a crime spree of some sort?"

"She thinks that she is an old fool and that you have been hiding behind her skirts to avoid the white men's agents and at the same time using her but loving Pansy."

"When Pansy picked me up on the road, she said the grandmother had sent her for me. She told me my name was Gray Feather and then brought me here. I had an extreme headache and couldn't think. I assumed she knew me and I just let her drive."

"Your answer, Gray Feather, is in that stack of old magazines. You go get them when the Cat fight starts. You may have to treat me for scratches and bites later."

"I have doctored many a dog after they have fought over females. I can handle it." He stated and then wondered why he had put his answer in those words.

"You are going to owe me, Gray Feather. I might want a roll in the hay with you as payment sometime in the future."

"I am Catholic, Running Deer, and believe that there is one woman out there for each man. I know Moon dance is that woman."

"I should be so lucky and Catholic. I have never had a man fall in love with me. I have had them lust after me.

"I have loved and lost and you want love but haven't found it. We would make good 'crying in your beer' buddies."

"I am tired of the Weelo, its culture, and its demands. I don't want to die old, leathered, and eating whatever I can catch in the desert. The money I make driving a truck could buy me a nice little cabin in the woods somewhere up north. I could have a refrigerator and a television. The women here live a harsh life. I know there is better out there and I want it. I feel guilty about my desire to abandon the tribe and it on verge of starvation most of the time. At the same time, I feel the men of the tribe should be out working and providing for their families instead of sitting in bullet trailers waiting for the Great Mother ship to come. I am a provider here, nothing more or nothing less. I make a paycheck and the tribe takes it from me giving me just enough money to eat on out on the road."

"So, this isn't a real reservation supported by the government?"

"Hell no, a cult is a better description. Three Toes, Wild Cat, North Star's husband, and I drive trucks and provide the money for the tribe to buy cornmeal and whatever else Grandmother Moon Dance feels the tribe needs. Our pay checks come home to the community. I am on a never ending long haul that I can't get off of. I want to."

"Every item the tribe has paid me with over the last three years has come out of the providers' pockets. You paid for all the chocolate bars I treated Moon Dance with. It should have been you eating them and Grandfather Night Shadow or me working to pay for her candy. I have really been blind and have taken my share of the purchased items never giving it a thought. I am an honorable man. I will get a job and pay you and the other providers back for the share I have taken and my paycheck will not come home to the tribe. It looks like I am making a sudden forced choice to abandon the tribe here today."

"I wish the other men in the tribe would have a light bulb moment. Take Pansy with you when you go to live in the white man's world. Since she has lost her weight, she is capable of making herself a good life working in one of the Indian casinos."

"Pansy is my friend and I will do my best to help her. I don't have a clue what she has pulled to make the tribe so angry, but I will not let the tribe harm her. She is a walking treasure of Weelo heritage and should relocate to a city somewhere and become a writer."

"I am glad you see something in her the others don't. She is low man on the totem pole here and the tribe will tire of her obsession with her Texas family and eventually force her to marry some old Weelo Indian fart who needs a nursemaid. I fear they will mate her with Night Shadow now that his boots have been set out."

"I know that Pansy Sky Walker is your child." Gray Feather replied. "Who is her father? I know she is obsessed with some man in Texas and his daughter. She talks about them, but never puts a name to them."

"I did something I shouldn't have done years ago and have paid for it dearly. I picked this white dude up who was outside the reservation on the main highway broke down. He had his car hood up and was trying to wave down someone to stop and help him. His name was Pete and he owed a processing plant down in Southern Texas. I was drunk, just in off the road, and was trying to chill out. He was well on his way to getting drunk also. We headed to Las Vegas in my semi and had a weekend long affair that I barely remember. Monday evening when we both sobered up in the bunk of my Semi we discovered a marriage license. We managed to get married Las Vegas style in spite of being drunk as skunks. I was newly pregnant at the time and was stressed out about. I told him the baby was his and left the tribe for about a year and stayed with him in Texas till after Pansy was born. I met this processing plant supervisor named Jose and ran off with him and a truck load of cattle that everyone there assumed I took across the border into Mexico. I left Pansy with him thinking she would be better off. I knew what a rough life it was for a woman in the tribe. Also, I didn't want her. She was a con-

119

ception from rape. She was not Pete's child."

"Does she know?"

"I have always felt she would be happier thinking she was white. I have hoped that she would walk away from the tribe and make a life for herself amongst them. She has no future in the tribe except to be someone's wife, sit in a bullet flyer, and literally go hungry?"

"Rejecting her has been your way of pushing her toward a possible better life."

"I may have pushed her right into a penitentiary. Whatever she had pulled in the land of the white man is serious enough that the Weelo may do away with her. After I sleep a couple more hours, I am pulling out and heading for Texas to intercept her and save her ass. I may not come back."

"May I go with you? There is no reason for me to stay here, now. Moon Dance doesn't want me and the men have it in for me. It sounds like exit time to me."

"Three Toes told me you agreed to do the respectful thing and marry Moon Dance so she would have someone to care for her in her old age."

"It was more than respect, Running Deer. I love her. It is a hard thing to swallow, her throwing me away."

"I guarantee you a roll in the hay with me will make you forget her. Go for the magazines. I have a catfight to start."

"Before we go, would you like to tell me who Pansy's father is and get it off your chest? I am an honorable man; I don't repeat what you and the other Weelo women tell me."

"Grandfather Night Shadow raped me when I was eighteen. I had just started driving. He climbed up into my truck to supposedly take a look at it. I was young and naïve. He threw me on the bunk and raped me. There was no one to turn to. Night Shadow and Moon Dance were gods to the tribe and had sons that would possibly move up and be chiefs. His getting banned from the tribe was the happiest day of my life. The men have disposed of him."

"That is why we haven't seen him for a few days?"

"The tribe voted and he is gone, dead possibly in the desert. You must leave here today or you may meet the Great Spirit that I personally don't believe in. He has never done anything for me."

"I will go with you." He replied with sad eyes. His world was ending.

"I must go get Pansy and prevent her from returning here."

The cat fight went off as planned and Gray Feather continued his morning readings after grabbing the box of magazines from the Hogan and shoving them up into the semi for safe keeping. While he counseled afterwards, he made mental note of the women who had showed him their friendship. He hoped someday to be able to repay their allegiance to him. Moon Dance was not on the list. When noon came, he dismissed the line of women stating he would return after lunch. Then, he made his way to Hissing Cat's for lunch and to get his hair braided. He hadn't spotted Moon Dance all morning and she wasn't in the Hogan when he retrieved the box of news magazines.

At Hissing Cat's trailer, he knocked. She opened the door and let him in. Then, she immediately shooed out the tribe girl that was her appointed helper. Seating himself at her feet, he turned his back to her and she started undoing his unkempt braid. She then started to comb his hair, part it, and braid it. He ate his lunch while she worked. She had it hot and waiting for him when he arrived. He devoured the steaming bowl of rabbit stew.

Between bites, he asked. "I seem to be in trouble with the tribe for some reason that I do not know. I am aware why every woman in the tribe has stood for hours to speak with me. You are a chief's wife, a woman of honor. May I ask what I have done for Moon Dance to kick me out and the tribe to be up at arms with me? I will right the wrong I have done. I just don't know what it is. I am an honorable man."

"Pansy Sky Walker is the reason and you are not Weelo. That is all that I can tell you." She stated. "Moon Dance cannot marry you because of it. I am your friend and that is why I have asked you here for lunch and a braiding. I am old and expect to die at any time and there is not another conceived baby form for me to enter. Our blood line must be the problem. How would you feel about mating with one of the younger women to produce an infant body? We would not expect you to marry her. She is a pure Weelo and understands our need for bodies to step into and travel in. You are a new strain of blood in the tribe and it might be the magic factor in our producing again."

"I have a running of the heart for Moon Dance. How could I possibly sleep with another?"

"North Star and Leaping Lizard are willing to carry a baby of yours."

"That would be adultery. Both have husbands. I am an honorable man and I cannot do what you ask. I believe in fidelity."

"I have presented Three Toes proposition to you. You have the right to say no."

"Three Toes asked you to present this idea to me of servicing the tribe's women like a gigolo?"

"Yes, he is looking for a way to keep you alive. Conception and babies are a priority right now. You are not Weelo as they have believed. You are human and disposable if the tribe votes that way. "

"How do you know that I am not Weelo? I don't even know who I am. My only memories are of the three years spent here in Moon Dance's lodge."

"Pansy Sky Walker brought you here telling us you were a medicine man from the north tribe. Moon Dance pulled a box of magazines from beneath her cabinet yesterday. Your photo in a white man's angel robe is on one of the covers. You are wanted by the white man."

"I honestly do not remember anything before my brain fog except flash memories of a big yellow dog with a cold black nose."

"Moon Dance cannot marry you and our tribe is at risk. They tribe will agree to let you remain with us and hide you if you agree to be a producer just as we have providers. We need infant bodies."

"You are asking me to be a male whore." He replied in shock.

I love her, Hissing Cat. There is something in her eyes that is fascinating. I can see another woman dwelling in her leathered body."

"We all have our positions in the tribe. After today, you will no longer be a medicine man and trusted with everyone's secrets." She replied finishing with his braiding.

"I cannot in good conscience do what you ask."

"Then, you must leave here at day's end and before midnight. I do not know what the men will decide, but we women have been told to be prepared to pack up and move at midnight. The tribe does not want government interference in our lives. Law enforcement knocking on our trailer doors could cause major problems for us. Your problem in the tribe cannot be fixed. You must leave or possibly be killed."

"I understand. Do you know how hard it will be for me to leave Moon Dance?"

"Time is a winter that kills the flowering bud of love. Your heart will be silent for awhile, but spring will come again and your heart will run once more. For now, you must enter a time of winter and flee for your life."

"I know that you had to be a great Chief's wife. You have been a great friend to me. You have proved it with your words telling me what you know. Moon Dance has chosen not to be my friend and that has greatly saddened my soul. I would like to ask permission of you to love you some future spring. My heart chose wrong and now it hurts. I must learn to choose like a Weelo. Three Toes gave me a choice of you or Moon Dance to Marry. I chose wrong and now he has claim to you for a wife."

"Three Toes can go to hell. Only an honorable man will share my bed. He has dishonored you as his friend not coming to you personally and asking you about the issue at hand. He trusts the white man's magazine and not your words and position of respect which you have earned. How can he be chief and not listen to you. Pansy Sky Walker, however, has given us multiple reasons over the years to disrespect her. She picks fights constantly with the Carlson family in Texas trying to claim a position in their white family tribe. She would dump us in a heartbeat to be accepted by them. Her willfully chosen part in the issue at hand may get her killed. The ultimate sin in the land of the Weelo is to bring law enforcement to our door."

"Whatever the problem is, Hissing Cat, I will not bring law enforcement here. I will leave with Running Deer about dark. She has a load going north. I am an honorable man. I will not send law enforcement knocking. I am sorry I have not spent time with you, a true friend. When the chips are down, you find out who your true friends are. Moon Dance has disrespected me in my time of need."

"Moon Dance is a fool choosing the tribe and its traditions over you. You are an honorable man. Many of our Weelo human men are not. Should the Great ship come before I pass over, I will choose you to take over with me. I want to go home on the arm of a man of respect. My husband, the chief, was a man of honor and respect. He was human but a believer in our words about the Great Mother ship. I was the ancient one in our pairing."

"I was a fool for choosing Moon Dance and not you. I now can see the great ancient one that lives in your eyes and body. Forgive me, Hissing Cat."

Gray Feather rose and returned to his last afternoon of counseling. He would read for two or three women and then claim to have a headache and go check out the box of magazines for clues to who he was and what his connection before his brain fog was to Pansy. They could have been a pair of criminals. He didn't know.

It was mid afternoon and Gray Feather was relieved to have his last sitter plop down on his sitter rug. After her, he was going to Running Deer's semi to look at the magazines. Running Deer was going to sleep till he returned. Gray Feather's mind was spinning and his legs had just about gone to sleep sitting cross legged so long. He took a deep breath and stretched while one of the Indian women tried to convince a five or six year old girl named Walks Crooked to take her turn. The men hadn't returned yet. The little girl sat down on the sitting rug, took her socks and shoes off, and stretched her feet out in front of her and proceeded to wiggle her toes ignoring him. She glanced over to one side at a Raven that was standing and pecking at something about twenty feet from her.

Gray Feather immediately asked her a question to get the women to quit fussing with her. It didn't matter to him if she crossed her legs Indian Fashion. His own crossed legs were killing him. He would give anything to stretch his legs out like her and wiggle his toes.

"My name is Gray Feather. What is your name?" he asked grinning at the cute little girl with long black hair and brown eyes just like the big yellow dog he sometimes had flashes of.

"My name is Walks Crooked." She said eyeing him and continuing to wiggle her toes."Why do you ask my name? We play catch all the time when you are not counseling. Howling Wolf says he can throw a ball faster than you. I told him you were the fastest and the best because you have the Great Spirit helping you with his magic."

"You are absolutely right, Walks Crooked. I shouldn't have asked you your name. You must remember that I have a brain fog and sometimes I don't remember things." He stated grinning and looking at her toes which hadn't stopped moving.

"Howling Wolf tells me you have a brain fog because you eat too many vegetables. He says a man has to eat meat to have brains. If you want, I will share my meat with you so you will know me the next time." She replied simply and continued to eye the bird.

"I am glad to know what has caused my loss of brains. You will be a great medicine woman someday and cure brainless old fools like me."

"No, I am not going to be a medicine woman. We already have one. I am going to be a school teacher and make all of my pupils wear pink dresses just like the fashion dolls the charity women brought me."

"You are even going to make the boys wear pink dresses?" he asked teasing her.

"The boys can wear purple shirts. I like that color to."

Gray Feather's Fog

"You will make a great teacher, but there will be brainless old medicine men like me who will need new brains and someone to tell them to eat meat to get them."

"Maybe I will reconsider if everyone wears pink when they come to sit on my rug."

"Do you have a question for the Great Spirit?"

"No, I am just wasting your time like my mother told me to do. She told me to ask you how to make vegetable lasagna, whatever that is. She said it was a long recipe and would kill my twenty minutes. Why are the women trying to keep you busy and out of the desert?"

"I am a really bad hunter. They are afraid I might shoot a rifle wrong and put a bullet thru one of the men accidentally." Gray Feather stated glancing over at the girl's mother who was plainly embarrassed.

"Howling Wolf is a good shot. They made him the guard to keep you away, should you follow. They told him to shoot you with his BB gun like a rabbit. Are you part rabbit? I have heard Pansy Sky Walker tell of your angel robe that hopped and zigzagged on its own in the dessert. Are you a hopping Jack Rabbit . . . or did my daddy call you a white federal Jackass? They sound alike."

At that point, the mother of Walks Crooked jerked her up off the sitter rug and pulled her out of sight scolding her.

125

CHAPTER SIXTEEN

GRAY FEATHER'S MEMORY RETURNS

Just after Gray Feather had finished with his last tribal woman needing counseling, an old car sped into camp causing a dust storm from its wheels. The tribe knew not to speed into camp making such an unwanted funnel of dust. The car stopped and Pansy Sky Walker exited carrying a shopping mall tote bag. She wasn't supposed to be back for a week. Gray Feather panicked as he watched the auto circle and leave. Apparently, she knew nothing of the trouble was brewing.

"Did Moon Dance throw you out?" she asked pleased at seeing him and his rug next to her Tee Pee. She set her tote bag of dirty clothes and personal items on the ground.

"Pansy, trouble is brewing. Don't question me. Just walk with me to the lover's dune. There is law enforcement at the camp's door and the tribe thinks we have caused it. Take my arm and act like we are glad to see each other. You and I have been kept in the dark. Our fate has been put to the tribe and voted on today."

"Oh shit . . ." she said. "Getting any type of law enforcement calling out here is considered the unforgiveable sin to the Weelo. She linked her arm in his and they sauntered towards the dune with Running Deer eyeing them sadly from a side window of her Semi truck. She thought for sure that Gray Feather had considered starting a relationship with her. Watching her daughter and him walk toward the lover's dune, she snapped. Starting up her truck, she pulled out of camp kissing the Weelo and her daughter goodbye forever. She had done her part as a provider and mother to a child that she didn't want who had just walked to the lover's dune with a man she did want. It was the breaking straw for her. Her life as a Weelo was over. She wouldn't return.

When out of hearing of the camp and behind the dune, Pansy asked. "What is up?"

"One of the women in the tribe found a magazine with a photo of two men on the front running in a church away from the altar. Both were dressed in angel robes like the one I discarded in the dessert. FBI agents are looking for one of the men and they say that man is me. I have no memory of anything except sitting in a street and you helping me into your car. The tribe recognized you standing in the crowd in the photo watching me run. Did you help me steal the wine and offering box that day from the church? I vaguely remember you telling me that when we were returning to the reservation."

Pansy had to think quickly to get out of this one and then plan an escape for her and him. She knew what the tribe did to men who brought trouble to their door. They killed them and disposed of their bodies in the desert.

"We did do it, Gray Feather and now we have got to get out of here when dark falls. The tribe will kill us for this offense. Did you say they voted today?" she asked thinking of her cad which wasn't running. Road Runner's motorcycle was their best choice for transportation. It didn't take much gas and they could go along way on the twenty or so dollars she had in her pocket. The last tribe member that brought FBI agents to the camp was taken far out into a remote part of the desert and left to die of thirst and starvation.

"They went to the desert this morning, if that answers your question. I wasn't asked to go along and vote. The women were told to keep me busy counseling while they voted on what to do about you and me. One of the younger wives secretly told me."

"We have about twenty four hours from the time they started the vote. They will hunt and make sure the women have food before marching us into the desert. Have they returned yet with food or anything?"

"No, they left out about breakfast time and I haven't seen hide or hair of them or any meat being brought back."

"The Road Runner's motorcycle is our best bet for transportation out of here. I have a key to it." She replied in a thinking mode. "Looks like I am going to be moving in with my father whether he likes it or not."

"That is something you and I are going to have to talk about when we get away from here."

"I hear someone coming, Gray Feather. Whoever it is won't bother us if we are making love. The tribe is desperate for babies to be born. Strip your shirt off and crawl on top of me. Whoever it is will turn and leave. The first lovers arriving here for the evening gets the dune for as long as needed."

Gray Feather jerked off his T-shirt, threw it on the ground, and climbed on top of Pansy pushing her skirt up with his hands and then pressing his lips to hers. They could hear whistling heading their way. Pansy, now 125 pounds and extremely nice looking, wrapped her arms around Gray Feather and moved her hands all over him listening to the whistling. She recognized the happy tune. Moon Dance whistled her babies to sleep instead of singing to them. Pansy had heard her whistles when she was a child and had listened to them when no one was rocking or putting her to sleep. She had often pretended she was in Moon Dance's arms and the whistling war for her nighttime pleasure. She was shuffled about amongst the tribe as an unwanted half breed baby.

Reaching the top of the sand dune and preparing to walk down over it, Moon Dance stopped in her tracks in shock. She had not expected to find Gray Feather making love to Pansy Sky Walker. Someone with a sadistic nature had told her that Gray Feather was beyond the dune waiting for her. She had wrestled all day with her love for him and her allegiance to the tribe. She had decided to leave with him and go secretly to the tribe in the north. What she saw broke her heart. His love for her was short lived and the friend who told her to meet him beyond the dune was not a friend.

As Gray Feather lay on top of Pansy listening and with his lips pressed to hers, he felt Pansy start putting her hands where she shouldn't. He hadn't been with a woman in three years and her hands and kisses were just too much for him. He gave in to the electricity of her touch and made love to her not knowing that Moon Dance stood in the night shadows watching with tears in her eyes. He also didn't see her walk away with a shattered heart.

An hour passed as Gray Feather and Pansy made love lying in the sand. When they were finished, they lay ringing wet holding each other. As they snuggled up to each other for warmth, Gray Feather stated, "You have made this Jersey boy one happy man. Your kisses are better than those of Carol Sue."

"What?" She asked raising her head off his arm and looking at him with a confused look on her face.

Gray Feather sat up with a strange look on his face and released Pansy from his arms with a thud.

"Oh shit!" He stated jumping up and grabbing for his jeans. The frenzied activity of making love had shaken loose his brain fog. All of his memories came flooding back. He turned and looked at Pansy who was lying naked in the sand.

"You were in the back of the church. You were trying to exit the same time we were. You had an inhaler in your hand. I ran past you. You have known all along that I am not Gray Feather but a member of Connie Carlson's wedding party. You saw my friend Ralph dump her at the altar. Why would you do this to me? You have made me believe I am someone that I am not. I am a doctor from New Jersey, an animal doctor. Why Pansy? I was just an innocent man who happened to be the best man to a fleeing groom."

She didn't answer for a moment.

"You aren't Connie's groom from New Jersey?"

"Hell no! My friend Ralph was her fiancé. I am Doctor Michael Haven not Doctor Ralph Archer. I am a vegetarian and an animal activist and halfway engaged to a nurse named Jennifer. Oh God. . ." he stated suddenly thinking of all of the animals he had eaten to survive. "You have caused me to have to eat meat for three years which is totally against my principals."

"You have to be Connie's fiancé." She replied in shock. "Connie spoke of her fiancé having a beer belly. I saw your thick waistline when I followed you. I did wonder how you managed to lose it so quickly."

"I am a doctor with a vegetarian girlfriend named Jennifer and I have a huge yellow Collie dog named Carol Sue. Oh God . . . Carol sue was expecting a litter of pups and I wasn't there for her."

"But I saw the best man take off in his red rental car."

"It was my rental car. I loaned it to Ralph to make his escape in. I ran the other direction drawing the attention away from him. I intended to call a cab from a convenience store that I had seen on the way to the church."

"I just seduced and slept with the best man?" she asked and then started laughing hysterically.

"I have been here three years . . . My dog . . . Ralph . . . my clinic . . . and all my pet owners that depended on me. You have stolen my life from me Pansy and let me sit here in the desert going hungry and doing without. Why?"

Pansy didn't answer but just continued to laugh like she had lost it.

Forgetting about both of their needs to flee, Michael grabbed his T-shirt and started running for the camp. Once there, he spotted Road Runner standing by his motorcycle talking to Hissing Cat outside her silver bullet shaped trailer. He ran up to him and demanded, "Let me have your keys. I am Doctor Michael Haven and I am going home." He then grabbed the keys from the hand of Road Runner and pushed him to the ground to gain access to the cycle. He then climbed on the motorcycle, kicked up the stand, and quickly inserted the key and started it.

Jo Hammers

Road Runner regained his footing and was about to jump Michael and fight him with a knife for the keys when an elderly arm grabbed his and held him back.

"Let him go. We will be out of here by midnight. You are the only one of the tribe who is brilliant and has a future should the Great Mother Ship fail to come for us. This is not the time to become a killer.

CHAPTER SEVENTEEN

HOME

Doctor Michael Haven, formerly Gray Feather, stood at his friend Ralph's door wondering what in the world he was going to say to explain his three year absence. He was ashamed that he had stood on street corners with cardboard signs begging to come up with the money for a bus ticket home. He had left the Road Runner's bike in the town nearest the reservation with a note on it saying who it belonged to. He wasn't a thief. He had made it home in the dead of winter with Jeans and a T-shirt on with an old shower curtain he had found in a trash can wrapped around him to shield him from the elements. He was home, but he was in poor condition.

It would have been easy to have made a phone call and asked Ralph or the police to help him get home. However, he had bonded with the Weelo people and he didn't want to leave a paper trail that would lead back to them. He intended to tell his friend and law enforcement that he had been a street person on the East coast till his fog cleared. He hated Pansy for stealing his life, but at the same time loved the Weelo. They were his family and he couldn't betray them, even though they were currently holding him in disrespect.

He had in his heart a list of which of the Weelo that had stood by him. He would send for any of them that wanted to relocate to a better life and take them into his lodge which would be a loft apartment. He had always been a sky dweller. His parents had lived in an apartment high in the sky and it was a way of life for him. He was sure that he could make a good life for himself and two or three of the Weelo who were willing. He was a doctor and he could hire them and train them making them self-sufficient. He was ashamed of himself for giving into a moment of lust and making love to Pansy. He was also ashamed of abandoning her when she needed his help. He didn't have a clue as to what her outcome of the voting day was.

Now he stood with a conscience that was ashamed and a body that wore rags.

He was barefoot, hungry, and at least a week without a bath or a shave. His hair hadn't been combed, washed, or braided since the morning Hissing Cat had done it. His fingernails were broken and dirty. A doctor would never be seen filthy like he was. He had scrounged to get home and here he was. He had eaten out of garbage cans and rode in the backs of trucks to leave no trail back to Moon Dance and the tribe. He barely had the strength to knock. He was thin on the reservation for lack of nourishing food and the long journey home had sapped his strength. His knees felt weak and rubbery.

As he stood at the door preparing to knock, he thought about Jennifer, the nurse he was dating when he disappeared. She was probably married. He didn't want to think about what might have happened to his dog. He hadn't told Ralph or anyone where he boarded her before leaving. The Kennel owner had probably sold her or gave her away when he didn't return. He was heartsick for his possible losses here and also those on the reservation. His biggest heart break was the loss of Moon Dance who had taken him in and cared for him for three years. Even though she had broken his heart, he could not betray her. She was that one special woman that comes along once in a lifetime that the Catholic nuns had said would come. He was Catholic and believed in fidelity. He would never love anyone but Moon Dance and was really ashamed of his casual one night affair with Pansy.

Raising the door clapper, he knocked ignoring the door bell. Years ago, he would have had a key. However, somewhere at the time of his brain fog he had lost his wallet and Ralph's key hidden in one of its compartments. He clapped the door knocker a second time and waited shivering. It was the first of January and there was snow on the ground. He heard a dog barking and the shuffle of feet the other side of the door. Then, the porch light flickered on. He took a breath in anticipation of facing his old life.

The door opened and he was surprised to see a very pregnant Jennifer standing there with a six month old baby on her hip and a two year old holding on to her knee. She immediately screamed and fainted. Michael grabbed the baby from her arms as she fell. The two year old started crying. Then he saw his friend Ralph come running to the door to see what the thud was and in shock he grabbed the door frame to hold himself up. Stepping over Jennifer, he threw his arms around his friend Michael Haven who was wrapped in a vinyl shower curtain and holding his baby.

"Oh my God . . . it is you!" Ralph stated breaking into sobs and ignoring the fainted woman on the floor who was starting to come to. "Where in the Hell have you been. It has been three years. I thought you were dead. You look dead." He stated stepping back and taking a look at Michael.

"I was dead, Ralph. After we left the church, I was running and somehow fell and hit my head. I have had a three year brain fog case of amnesia. I have been wondering around the coast as a street person. On Christmas day, my memories came flooding back. I remembered you and where home is. I didn't have any money, so I have hitch-hiked back home to you. I am sorry I am so dirty and look so bad."

"You should have called me collect. I would have flown to where you were and brought you home."

"I still have a little fog and can't remember phone numbers." He stated lying to protect the tribe. "I have just focused on getting home. I am going to have to be seen by a doctor tomorrow. I fear that my brain fog amnesia will return. Don't let me wander off again, Ralph. Please don't lose me." Michael stated and began to cry.

"Come on in, buddy. We will cry together. I personally am giving you a hot tick and flea dip bath and cleaning you up. I guarantee you I won't let you wander off again. I have never been so glad to see anyone in my whole life. The FBI found your angel robe in the New Mexico desert. They have you in a cold case file believing you to be dead and eaten by wild animals. How did you end up back on the East coast?"

"I don't exactly remember. I think some tourist picked me up and gave me a ride west and then another one picked me up and took me East. I was just glad to be in a car and riding. I had no memory and a terrible headache that lasted for days. I have been a street person with no ID or memories. I have slept in culverts and on beaches. I headed home to you, Jennifer, and Carol Sue as soon as my memory returned."

"Jennifer is an item that you and I are going to have to discuss. A few changes have occurred since you disappeared."

"I can see that. I gather that the two of you are now a couple."

"We found each other in our grief over you. We have two children and as you can see, a third on the way. The baby is Michele and the toddler is Michael. We named him after you."

Michael stooped down and eyed the crying little two year old Jersey boy with the typical Italian dark hair. "Your dad and I are best friends. You are going to be my second best friend."

Ralph helped Jennifer to her feet.

"I . . . I . . . don't know what to say," She stated reaching out to hug the dirty, disheveled Doctor Michael Haven.

"It is okay, Jennifer. I am sorry that I didn't come back. I have had amnesia from a fall. My memory came back Christmas day. I hitchhiked home. I couldn't remember phone numbers or street addresses. I am still a little fuzzy on some things."

"I have two children, Michael. I didn't intend to abandon you as dead and marry your best friend. Loving Ralph just happened. I don't know what to say."

"It is okay, Jennifer. I have had a lady friend, or did have a lady friend. I left her behind to make my way home. I didn't intentionally dump you for her. I did what I had to do to survive and she was part of that world. I have had amnesia from a fall. I am going to check myself into the hospital tomorrow. I don't want the memory loss to return. I want you and Ralph to keep tabs on me for awhile. I am frightened of losing my memory again."

"I understand," she replied. "Come on in. You can tell me about your lady friend when you feel up to it. Was she a vegetarian?"

About that time, a familiar yellow haired collie came running to the door barking and snarling at Michael.

Michael went to crying and stooped in hopes Carol Sue would recognize him. He had been gone so long and he didn't look like the clean cut animal doctor that she had once known. He held his hand out to her, but she backed away snarling.

"Carol Sue!" Ralph said roughly to her. The dog backed off down the entry hallway and left Michael standing in tears.

"I am sorry Michael. I paid the kennel bill on your dog after doing some serious searching for her. I brought her home here and she has become our family dog. Give her time."

"I have lived a life in a dark hole that wasn't me. Help me find my way back to you, Carol Sue, and to who I once was."

"You don't know how sorry I am about the Connie Carlson fiasco."

"Don't be sorry, Ralph. Be thankful you had the courage to run. I could have fell and hit my head when we were skiing or rock climbing and caused the same amnesia damage to myself. I just happened to hit my head in Texas and suffered memory loss. It could have happened on any of our adventures. The one good thing coming from it is that I am no longer afraid of water. I slept by, swam in, and bathed in a hole of water where I was. The brain fog took care of my phobia."

"Jennifer, show him to the guest room and then get him some pajamas and a robe from my closet. I am giving this old dog, my friend a much needed bath and then I am feeding him everything green or fruity in our refrigerator. Call and order us in a vegetable pizza."

"Thank you Ralph," Michael stated in a weak state. I need you."

"Tonight, I will clean you up and feed you. Tomorrow, I will go with you to the hospital and stay with you while you get checked over. For now, you are getting a hot Jacuzzi bath, a clean bed, all the vegetables you can eat, and my two kids to drive you crazy with their whining."

"What happened to Carol Sue's litter of pups?" Michael asked thinking perhaps he could buy one of them back somewhere.

"She lost the pups according to the kennel owner. It took me two months to find her. I am sorry."

"Thank you for going and finding her. You know what she means to me. It is okay with me that she has bonded with you and the kids."

Michael turned to Jennifer who had taken him by the arm and was helping him down her hallway toward the guest room.

"I am glad you are back. You do know that you and I . . . "She stated not finishing her sentence."I am sorry about us."

"I am happy for you Jennifer. Ralph has always wanted a house full of kids."

For the next year, Michael Haven readjusted to his world as a veterinarian. Being older, he gave up the night life of the rock clubs he once lived and breathed to play the guitar in. His desire for flashing lights and the college age club scene was gone. Survival in the desert had given him a different set of priorities. He tried desperately to reconnect with carol Sue, but the dog refused to have anything to do with him. He did not get another dog because he feared losing his memory again and going off and leaving another innocent animal to fend for itself. His biggest ordeal in returning home was dealing with his memories of Pansy and Moon Dance. He couldn't talk about them for fear of law enforcement charging the tribe with kidnapping. He pushed the thoughts of them as far down into a dark pit of forgetting as he could get them where the sun didn't shine. He told everyone that he had been a street person and never spoke of his experience in detail with anyone and that Included Ralph. There were no street person memories.

The day after Michael returned home, Ralph called the FBI and the Carlson family informing them that Michael had been found. Connie and Pete Carlson were thrilled to get the FBI off their backs and there was no further communication between them and Ralph.

Three years passed. Doctor Michael Haven resumed his life as a vegetarian and a vet. However, he was not the same. Inside he was Weelo and missed the tribe that he had bonded with. At the same time, he knew he could never go back. Moon Dance had disrespected him and the men of the tribe, his friends, had intended to possibly kill him. Even if he wanted to go home to the Weelo, he couldn't. Inside he felt like a walking Zombie. He was smiling and functioning on the outside, but inside where it counted, he felt dead. Winter had indeed killed the bud of life in his soul and he saw no hints of spring.

It was the first week in January and Doctor Ralph Archer had been on an extended drinking binge and was to be released from a psychiatric hospital where he had been sent by Jennifer to dry out. Michael stood in the office of Ralph's psychiatrist, Doctor Jack Benson who was also his psychiatrist. He had come to pick up Ralph who had been a month long resident in the mental health facility. Ralph had drunk himself into a stupor and then attempted to kill himself by running into a tree. Michael and Dr. Benson were in the middle of a conversation while the nurse was getting Ralph packed up and ready to be dismissed.

"Ralph is going to be successful, sooner or later Michael. You have got to convince him that you do not want Jennifer and his children. He married her when you were missing and he is guilty thinking he betrayed you with her."

"I don't want Jennifer. You know that I am in love with someone else that I just can't bring myself to speak about with Ralph or anyone."

"I am your psychiatrist as well as Ralph's. I understand your need to keep Moon Dance and the tribe a secret. Are you willing to let Ralph kill himself because you have a secret of loving a seventy some year old woman and a tribe of cult Indians?"

"My secret will make me look like a fool. I was in love with a woman that was three times my age and made love to my kidnapper. I am ashamed of who I was when I was missing. I ate meat and lived a life that was not me. How do I tell Ralph that I sat outside a Hogan and counseled an Indian tribe thinking I was Gray Feather, a medicine man? I am still in love with the leathered, tooth missing, medicine woman named Moon Dance. The experience has warped me. I can't admit to being the gullible, naïve, fool I was."

"If you love your friend, as you say, you will tell him about Pansy and Moon Dance so he doesn't see you as hating him for marrying Jennifer."

"I have kept Pansy Sky Walker a secret to keep her from being arrested for kidnapping me. I didn't even know that she had kidnapped me. I was in a brain fog. How do I explain making love to a kidnapper?"

"There are things left unsaid in your life. You need to move forward and let Ralph be a friend to you and grieve with you over the loss of Moon Dance. Ralph needs to see you as human and a failure in the relationship department like him. He sees you as a returned god and himself as a miserable heel of a pervert having married Jennifer and had kids by her. "

"I am far from being a God, although the Weelo were convinced that I was a medicine man who spoke to their Great Spirit. I actually believed I was a medicine man who spoke to the Great Spirit till my memories came flooding back."

"Ralph is going to commit suicide if you don't help him, Michael. Is your embarrassment over loving a much older woman and sitting on a rug telling fortunes more important that Ralph's life?"

"You are right. However, I don't know how to even begin to tell him about Moon Dance or making love to my kidnapper. I used to rib him big time about his Texas Two Stepping Connie Carlson. I talked him into dumping his Texas fiancé."

"Is his life worth a little ribbing?" Jack Benson asked.

"I am ashamed of the three years, my eating of meat, and loving Moon Dance. Men here would call me a thirty year old pervert for fooling with a grandmother. I am afraid Ralph will see me as less of a man and a friend. I can never go back to the Weelo, so why talk about it?"

"I am asking you to take Ralph with you to the reservation and let him see you as less than perfect. He went thru as much trauma as you did when you disappeared. I think you owe him closure. He will understand the change in you if he knows where and how you lived during that time. He thinks you have changed because of Jennifer. Neither of you are the young men who once partied, vacationed, and did stupid young stuff together. You can't be those youthful, naïve, carefree, young men again. Your stupid stuff days are over and you both live with adult demons. You have got to find your way back to each other as friends, but in a new way. He feels guilty for having married your girlfriend and alienated you from your dog. Jennifer has asked him for a divorce. That is the reason for his current drinking binge. He thinks she is still in love with you and that he has been a fool. He looks at his children and thinks they should be yours."

"I have no intention of pursuing Jennifer. If anything, my experience in the desert showed me I was not in love with her. I would have married Moon Dance. I loved her and still do. I will admit that I was thinking of marry Jennifer before my brain fog. I saw us compatible because of our both being vegetarians and our shared interests in animal rights. It wouldn't have worked out. We didn't love each other. Moon Dance is the other half of my heart. I am glad Ralph and Jennifer found each other."

"Ralph is going thru an alcoholic hell that is as devastating as the three years you spent in a brain fog. You have got to help him find his way home to you. The two of you lost the years when friends smoke cigars and congratulate each other on the births of children. Ralph needs to know that you loved a woman out there at the same time he was making love to Jennifer and having babies with her. He needs to see you as human and not some god that has came back from the grave that he has disrespected. He is even guilty about your dog having bonded with his children."

"I am afraid if I go back I will take one look at Moon Dance and not return here. I am nothing there. I am somebody here. I am me. Gray Feather there was a phony."

"Did you know that one of my passions is Indian Folk Lore? I would love to make a trip to the southwest and meet the story teller that you call Pansy. Suppose I go along to be there for you and Ralph. We could make a three friend trip. I would be there if either of you should need me and I could indulge my passion for folk lore at the same time. I have been reading an Army Captain's journal written in the 1800s that tells of a tribe who believed that a great mother ship like Noah's Ark, was coming for them. I would love to talk to your storyteller and discuss with her the captain's writings. You, actually, should write a book about your experience with the odd Indian tribe. I bet you could even get a movie deal for your story."

"What would I title the book, Gray Feather's Brain Fog?" Michael asked sarcastically.

"To you, Michael, it may have been a brain fog. However, did it ever occur to you that you might have experienced some sort of paranormal event?"

"My office staff thinks I am crazy and Ralph says I am not the same as I used to be. Writing about the three and one half years could label me a permanent fruit cake. I dream of going home to Moon Dance and feeding her chocolates. She may be dead now. She would be seventy-six or seventy-eight now. I know she is close to eighty."

"Think about what I have said, Michael. Ralph needs you! The time is now or you are going to be picking your friend up at the morgue and burying him."

"You and Ralph will end up just as crazy as I am if we make a trip to the Weelo reservation. I now sleep on a rug on the floor beneath my apartment window just so I can pretend I am in the bed with Moon Dance. I am here in New Jersey, but the Michael I was before the Bullhorn, Texas fiasco is gone forever. I am functioning as a doctor here and want the conveniences I have here. However, I am Gray Feather on the inside and I love Moon Dance and the life I had with her in the desert of New Mexico. I know I can't have it both ways and that my life in New Jersey is the better choice. Also, I cannot forget Moon Dance discarded me. I don't have her to go back to. So, I sleep on a rug beneath my kitchen window and pretend I am back in the three years when she loved me. It doesn't get any crazier than that."

Michael took his friend Ralph Archer home only to have to call paramedics two weeks later due to Ralph taking a bottle of sleeping pills. The words of his and Ralph's psychiatrist broke the silence barrier in Doctor Michael Haven's heart. He couldn't let his friend die. He remembered how Ralph had bathed him like he was a little baby when he half collapsed having made it home. He had lifted him in and out of the bathtub and hand fed him. It was payback time, even if it cost him his dignity.

CHAPTER EIGHTEEN

TICKETS TO THE PAST

After much soul searching, Michael felt that Jack, his friend and psychiatrist, was right. Ralph was spiraling down and it was up to him to do something about it. The veterinary clinic closed its doors for a week of vacation at Easter time. Michael purchased three tickets to Ft. Worth, Texas. From there, he would make a journey with Ralph and Jack as support to the church in Bullhorn, Texas and then retrace his journey into the land of the Weelo. He had sat down with Ralph and Jack two weeks prior and related his story telling Ralph how ashamed he had been of who he was after his memory returned and the fact that he had been in love with a seventy some year old woman. Ralph seemed to enjoying seeing his friend as vulnerable and a victim like it was bringing a closure to an event that had never made sense to him. Ralph got a real charge out of hearing the story about the zig-zag moving angel robe with the goose wings on the back and the part about him and Pansy jumping into the old green cad frightened thinking the Great Spirit had sent a goose spirit to scare them. He asked several times how big Pansy was as thought it brought some sort of satisfaction to him. They had always been studs who dated skinny bikini beach or ski slope girls. Michael in particular had a preference for red heads and blondes and never dated a girl that wasn't gorgeous. He had always been handsome and a chic magnet that only dated a girl that he considered to be a ten. More than once he had told Ralph that Connie Carlson was a possible two. He had ruthlessly ribbed Ralph about his redneck, bleached blonde, Texas two stepping bimbo. Now it was his turn.

So, three male studs and friends from New Jersey, all doctors, stood in the desert in New Mexico leaning on a rental car viewing the spot where Michael had thrown away his goose winged best man's robe.

"A three hundred and fifty pound Indian woman, named Pansy Sky Walker, drove you out here in your angel winged robe and convinced you that you were an Indian tribe medicine man?" Ralph asked breaking out into laughter remembering who Michael used to be. Michael had talked him out of marrying the petite Connie Carlson.

"I looked at her and decided I was a man who was attracted to big women." Michael replied biting his lip knowing that Ralph needed to see him as loving someone besides Jennifer."

"And you made love to her?" Ralph inquired laughing and looking out onto the dessert loving the story.

"As crazy as it seems, Ralph, yes it happened. I fell, hit my head, and didn't remember my old life with you and Carol Sue for over three years. I was making love with Pansy, the three hundred and fifty pound Indian woman my age when my memory came back. I didn't have a clue that I was Italian or from New Jersey or that I dated redheads. I was a blank slate and she pleased me."

"You didn't have any inkling that Jennifer was back home waiting for you?"

"Her name never crossed my mind. I saw the Indian woman and I wanted her. I think I have always had a screw loose, but just didn't want to admit it. There was a feather in my hair and Pansy Sky Walker told me I had been on a drunk and that was the reason for my loss of memory. I believed her. The braid and the feather said I was an Indian. Somewhere, down inside me, is a man that is attracted to women that are not redheads, blondes, or considered beautiful. Don't kill me for saying this, but in my thinking Jennifer is a dog next to Pansy and Moon Dance. In my fog, I learned what I really wanted in a woman and it wasn't a red or blonde headed bimbos like we used to date. In case you have forgotten, I met Jennifer on spring break at the beach. She is a cookie cutter of all the bikini girls we dated. Here, in New Mexico with a blank slate mind, I found two women who were not cookie cutters and I was smitten with them. They were real women."

The three friends walked a short way out into the desert bringing closure to that part of Michael's secret. Jack Benson, their psychiatrist just let them talk and he photographed their journey making mental notes of Michael's story going with his camera shots.

The landscape hadn't changed. Michael half way expected one of the tribe to come driving up the road in one of their beat up old pickups or perhaps one of the providers driving one of the tribe's four semi-trucks. However, the road into the dessert was silent. He remembered the ritual he and Pansy had performed and bit his lip at how utterly naïve and ridiculous he must have sounded back then. She was Connie Carlson's sister and had one thing in mind, to take and keep a man she thought was Connie's groom and lover. He wanted to cry, but he held it back. Ralph was too fragile for him to show weakness and turn back. He was not sure he had the courage to face the tribe and Moon Dance if she was alive. Jack was carrying a handgun and mace in case any of the men in the tribe gave them any problem. Gray Feather did not know what to expect.

Jo Hammers

"About ten miles further down this back road is the reservation, Ralph. I don't know whether they will be happy to see me or ask us to leave. I actually stole a motorcycle from them the night I left. The men were out for my hide and what friends I had were women."

"That figures. Women have always been attracted to you like you are a god. Jennifer cried when you came up missing. She has never cried over my ass."

"She was crying, Ralph, because my missing was a tragedy, not because there was anything between us. If it makes any difference to you, I had another girl-friend across the city that the two of you didn't know about." He stated lying for his friend's sake. "It was her that I planned to give the engagement ring to, not Jennifer. I planned to tell Jennifer when I returned from Texas that I was seeing someone else. I just didn't get the chance. The woman, I intended to give the ring to, was married. I was trying to coax her to leave her husband with the ring. I am sure that she didn't come forward when I was missing for fear of her husband getting custody of her child. I was going to marry a woman with a child. She wasn't even Catholic, Ralph."

"The ring in your suitcase that Jennifer wore for the three years you were missing was not for her?"

"No, it was for a woman named Cynthia who was a teacher and married. I met her at a charity fund raiser and thought I was in love with her. Now, I know I wasn't. Moon Dance is the love of my life and the only woman that I will ever love. Jennifer can have the ring. I haven't had the heart to tell her that it was intended for someone else."

"I married Jennifer when I was drunk and stressed out over your disappearance. I don't love her. I have children by a woman I don't love and have had guilt feelings thinking I married someone that you did love. Is it alright with you if I get a divorce and find myself a Moon Dance?"

"I am sorry that you have felt that I was in love with Jennifer and wanted her and your children. I have been ashamed to tell you that I was and still am in love with a seventy some year old medicine woman. I thought you would see me as a pervert and not the man I once was. I have been ashamed to tell you of my life as Gray Feather and the trick Pansy played on me convincing me I was someone that I was not. You and I have always been friends, but we also have been competitive. You date a blonde and I have to find one just a little bit blonder. Jennifer was my competition girl to match that vegetarian cook book writer from Maine you were seeing. I dated Jennifer for all the wrong reasons."

"Did you have any memories of Carol Sue?" Ralph asked.

142

"I appreciate your going and finding her. I had no recollections of her till the night my memories came back. The tribe had a dog named White Paws and I loved him. He was actually owned by a Weelo Indian boy named Howling Wolf. However, the dog slept with me every night on my rug in the grandmother's lodge. Howling Wolf's parents wouldn't let him have White Paws inside at night. He was just as much my dog as he was Howling Wolf's. I am thankful you took Carol Sue. I was bonding with another dog just as you and your children did mine. I couldn't bring White Paws with me because it would have broken Howling Wolf's heart."

"Which dog did you love the most?" Ralph asked.

Taking a breath, Michael lied because he knew that his friend needed to hear it. "I loved White Paws with everything in me because he and Pansy were all I had. I loved the Indian dog the most."

Ralph Smiled. "That is a relief. Your dog Carol Sue was all that kept me going for awhile when you disappeared. I didn't expect myself and my children to get so attached to her and vice versa. My children love your dog, Michael."

"I am happy about that, Ralph. Our lives took different paths for awhile but we are still the same friends we have always been. We just have a few years of separate memories. It wouldn't be any different than one of going off to war for two or three years. We would be changed by the years, but still be friends. I have shell shock and I am trying to find my way back. I am depending on you to not let me go crazy." Michael stated trying to help his friend.

"Being here is letting me see a side of you that I never knew." Ralph stated. "In a way, I am glad it happened to you. I would give my eye teeth to love a Moon Dance and have her love me."

"It is time for you and me to take our place in the world as men and not two young Jackasses intent on thrills and activities that are self serving. We are not kids anymore and the days of dating blondes and nit-wits are over. It is time for us to consider what is really important to us and pursue it. I am a doctor and your friend. Beyond that, I am going to create a new life for myself. I don't want the ski slope stud lifestyle I once had. I want a real life with a real woman's arms around me at night. You have children and I want to be a part of their life, not because I wish they were mine. I want to be part of their life because they are yours. In the same respect, should I have children, I want you to be there for them. I want you to know the real me, the man that has discovered he is able to love someone that is not a ten.

"Don't laugh, at the time I married Jennifer, I was smitten with a lady truck driver that delivered our pet supplies. She was as ugly as sin and had a set of hips on her that were out of control. She definitely needed a girdle. Anyway, there was something about her laugh that pleased me. If I hadn't got drunk and married Jennifer, I might have ended up with her. You were gone and I had no reason to date a bimbo. You are right. It is time for us to ask ourselves what we really want out of life and find arms of our choosing to hold us."

"Here, I brought something for this occasion," Michael stated handing Ralph a cigar. "We are celebrating our new birth and to the men we are becoming."

"I don't smoke," Ralph stated taking the cigar and turning it over in his fingers looking at it.

"Neither do I," laughed Michael, "However, today we are going to be sick as a dog, cigar smoking fools."

Michael pulled a lighter from his pocket and lit Ralph's after he bit the end off. Then he lit his own, inhaled, coughed, gagged, and spit.

"So much for us being men, we sound like a couple of thirteen year old first time cigarette smokers." Ralph stated laughing and coughing.

"I am your friend that went off to war and then returned. I have some battle scars. However, I am still the same friend to you I once was. The same goes for you. We have both been scared by the war, but now we have to pick up the pieces and find our way home to each other. I have post traumatic syndrome from the war. You have problems from gunshot wound to the chest. The women we loved have presented us with Dear John letters. It doesn't matter. We have each other as family. We are brothers as well as friends and will always be there for each other. Before the war we were young assholes that partied knowing nothing about the real world and life. After the war, we are men of honor and no longer stupid young jackasses. We know what we want and it isn't blonde bimbos and beer keg parties."

"You are right, Michael. Neither of us can help the war we accidentally joined and fought in. However, the war is over. Is it okay with you if I get a divorce" I know you are Catholic and believe it is one woman for a lifetime. I married Jennifer one night when she and I both were drunk as skunks. I want to reclaim who I was before Jennifer."

"It is okay, Ralph as long as you maintain a relationship with your children. Somewhere during my time with the Weelo, I became more liberal in my thinking. I converted and am now Weelo, not Catholic."

"A relationship with my children is not going to be a problem. Jennifer is giving me custody. She never wanted children. Having kids was my idea. I was trying to replace you."

"The two men hugged each other for a moment and then threw their cigars down, stomped them out, and got back into the rental car to drive the last ten miles to the reservation. They were finding their way home to each other as men.

Jack Benson just listened and continued to photograph their journey. He was a hoping to come up with something new in the way of Indian culture and folk lore that he could write a book about. He had an obsession and a feeling that he was being drawn to the experience that lay just ahead of them. He felt like he was following an invisible pied piper that was calling to him from the land of the Weelo. He couldn't explain the sound in his head that was like the singing on a piece of crystal when tapped.

The three men got back in their rental car and headed toward Gray Feather's memories of the Weelo and the reservation. Michael was excited as well as fearful of entering the camp and approaching the tribe. He was sure they would all be angry at him for taking Road Runner's motorcycle. He hoped the cycle had made its way back to them. If not, he would buy Road Runner another one. He wondered what Pansy's fate with the tribe was. Most of all, he hoped to catch just one last glimpse of Moon Dance. He still could not deal with the fact that she had discarded him so easily. He was sure that she was the only woman he would ever love. He had his demons to deal with and a shattered heart to mend.

Michael drove slowly. A part of him wanted to run like a deer towards Moon Dance, fall at her feet, and beg her to love him again. Another part of him remembered the women who showed their allegiance to him. A third part of him, the human part, wanted to turn the car around and forget everything concerning his three years in the desert. Pansy had stolen three years of his life. He wasn't sure how many of the tribe knew what Pansy had done. He wondered if Moon Dance had known that Pansy kidnapped him. If so, he had made a three year fool out of himself. He was sure that Ralph didn't realize the mental hell he was going thru to save him from alcoholism and suicide.

As he neared the Weelo encampment, he knew instantly something had happened. The silver bullet shaped travel trailers were gone. He entered the camp driving slowly. All that remained in the dessert was Pansy's rusty old Cadillac. Her Tee-Pee was gone. The Hogan was half burned down and looked like it had been abandoned for a long time. He pulled up slowly and parked in front of its door.

"This is it?" Ralph asked in a shocked voice. "This old Indian Hogan hasn't been lived in for years. There is no roof on it and the windows are gone."

"I don't know what has happened," Michael stated in disbelief as he exited the gray four door rental. "I swear to the both of you that there was a camp of Weelo Indians here and I lived with them. That is Pansy's old Cadillac out in the field."

"Michael," stated Jack Benson his psychiatrist and friend. "This place has been abandoned for at least a century if not more. No one could live in this harsh environment. There is no water source that I can see and no bullet shaped travel trailers as you have indicated. You may have been hallucinating."

"Jack, I swear to you that there was a village here with real people. The spring in the desert they drank from is just over that hill." He stated."Follow me and I will show it to you."

"Lead the way. I want you to be satisfied with your confrontation of your life here." Jack Benson stated and then proceeded to follow Michael a quarter of a mile out into the desert.

Ralph Archer stayed behind eyeing the old Cadillac and the Hogan that Michael referred to as the home of Moon Dance. He wondered if Michael had somehow imagined the Weelo story he told. He walked out to the old Cadillac and checked the glove box. Michael had been insistent that Pansy Sky Walker had kept it full of cookies and tiny bottles of perfume. The box was rusted and there was no sign of any collection of small glass flasks. He walked around to the back of the vehicle where the trunk was popped open. He pulled it open and a giant lizard came scampering out. He jumped back for a moment thinking it was a snake. Grinning, he stepped back up to the trunk and looked inside. There was nothing there but a flat spare tire and a can of oil that was probably fifty years old. The can was rusted out and the oil had long ago leaked out. He left the Cadillac and wandered back to the Hogan with the intent of digging around with a stick in the ruins to see if there were any artifacts.

Out in the desert, Michael led Jack Benson to the tiny hole of water that was now about three feet in diameter and had a dead raven floating in it. The hand dug swimming hole where the drinking spring spilt over into was gone.

"I am not crazy, see?" stated Michael pointing to the tiny spring. "It used to be bigger. The Weelo men kept it dug and cleaned out. Also, that dried up saucer shape in the sand was a handmade swimming and bathing pool. The men kept it dug out and the spring fed it."

"You drank for three years from that?" Dr. Jack Benson asked in shock. The water hole was visibly contaminated.

"The whole tribe drank from it. There was enough daily activity at the spring that there were no floating dead animals in it. Pansy and I made love over there beyond that small sand dune. That is where my memory came back."

"Let us walk over there, so you will be satisfied when we return to New Jersey." Jack Benson stated remembering all of Michael's stories of the Weelo and his night with Pansy.

Michael headed for the dune and walked up and over to the backside of it. He wasn't wrong or delusional. He looked at their spot in the sand and recalled the pleasure of making love after three years of not having a woman. He had been an animal. Then he recalled the horror when his memory returned and he realized Pansy had used and tricked him. A tear rolled out of his eye and down his cheek. "I swear, Jack. Pansy and I made love right here. This was also the spot where my memories returned."

"It is okay, Michael. It is time to return to the car. Ralph is going to get antsy and start blowing the car horn."

CHAPTER NINETEEN

RALPH LONG LEGS' DIVORCE

Meanwhile, back at the non-existent Weelo camp, Doctor Ralph Archer walked back toward the Hogan like structure with the intention of doing some poking around in the rubble for a possible artifact. Stepping to the door of the roofless structure, he peeped inside looking for more lizards or other creepy crawlers such as tarantulas. He was a city boy and not too fond of spiders, snakes, or scorpions. He wasn't too fond of the fleas he killed on the animals brought to him in the veterinarian clinic. He had a wimpy side that he never let anyone see.

Just as he stuck his head inside, he heard a rattling noise behind him. "Oh shit." He muttered turning around slowly knowing a huge snake had to be right behind him. Then he screamed like a girl. There was a snake alright and it was being held live by the neck by a weathered old woman who had to be at least eighty. The tail of the snake was curling and rattling. She held it out and to one side dangling like it was a piece of short rope. The snake's mouth was open and displaying its fangs.

"Don't move lady. You have a snake in your hand. On the count of three, throw it quickly into the desert away from us." Ralph stated in total shock and fright. The snake was no more than three feet from him and he had nothing to euthanize it with.

"Why would I do that, Long Legs? I just caught him. He will be my dinner tonight."

"Don't you think that you should have killed him before picking him up?" He replied backing up as far as he could from the old woman with part of her upper teeth missing.

"I do not have refrigeration like the white man does. I will keep him in a sack till evening falls and then kill him just before I cook him."

"Oh . . . that sounds logical." He replied staying back as far as possible.

"Who are you, Long Legs?" She asked walking over to the side of the Hogan and dropping the snake down into an old weathered gunny sack that might have held potatoes or meal at one time or another."

"I am Doctor Ralph Archer from New Jersey," He replied watching the sack move a little as she secured the top.

"You are a New Jersey doctor?" She asked suddenly smiling.

"Yes." He replied simply keeping an eye on the moving sack.

"Do you by any chance know our medicine man, Gray Feather? He left us suddenly and went home to the land of New Jersey."

"Are you Moon Dance?" He asked realizing his friend wasn't entirely crazy, just possibly touched a little.

"I am Moon Dance." She stated smiling exposing the fact that some of her upper teeth were missing. I once loved our medicine man, named Gray Feather till I walked over the sand dune and found him in the arms of Pansy Sky Walker. His love for me was not real. The animal in him chose Pansy."

"That sounds like Michael. He has loved his share of women including my wife."

"I am sorry. Did Gray Feather take her from you?"

"I took her from him while he was gone in a brain fog. I was told he was dead and I thought I was doing the right thing marrying and loving the woman he left behind."

"What is her name?"

"Jennifer."

"Ralph is too short of a name for a tall good looking medicine man like you. I will call you Ralph Long Legs. It fits you."

"Did you name my friend Gray Feather?" he asked smiling and wondering what his friend had seen in the gray haired, leathered old woman.

"Pansy named him. Why have you come here, Ralph Long Legs?"

"My friend Michael has brains that have been scrambled like eggs. He goes regularly to a medicine man in New Jersey that reads minds. We have returned here with him to find out if he is telling us the truth about a tribe of Weelo people or if he is crazy." he replied considering that she was way too skinny. Her bones were showing thru her skin.

Jo Hammers

"He slept beneath my kitchen window and sat here by the door counseling our tribe. He was a great medicine man during the time he spent with us. The tribe has moved to a new land. Pansy Sky Walker and Gray Feather brought trouble to our door and the Weelo have fled. If you are law enforcement, I am not afraid of you."

"I am not law enforcement. I am a medicine man like Gray Feather."

"The night Gray Feather left us; the tribe set my Hogan on fire. The Great Spirit sent a great rain to put the flames out just after they left. The roof is gone. Only the adobe walls remain. I saved enough items to be able to survive here. I now live beyond the lover's dune in Pansy Sky Walker's Tee Pee."

"I am glad to know that you are alive, real, and well. Michael speaks fondly of you."

"How is Gray Feather? Does he sleep now beneath the quilt of your wife?" She asked sarcastically with a very sad face.

"My wife loves him, but he does not sleep with her. He dreams of you and is ashamed of a night he spent in disrespect on the lover's dune. He says you discarded him and he was very lonely. It is not the arms of Pansy Sky Walker that he dreams about."

"Where is Gray Feather?" she asked with mixed emotions visible in her face.

"He went for a walk in the desert to your spring of water. He is with a doctor friend of ours named Jack Benson."

Moon Dance broke out in a grin. "Benson is with you"

"Do you know Jack Benson?" he asked in shock.

"We have been waiting for him to come. He is the lost member of our Weelo tribe. Hissing Cat has seen him in visions. North Star sees one of our ancient ones coming to us from the bottom of a bottle. Benson coming means the Great Mother Ship is near. Where is he?" she asked with a look of excitement crossing her face.

Ignoring her question, he asked, "Are you alone here?"

"A few women refused to go to the land of Utah and hide out as one of many wives of a Joseph follower. Pansy Sky Walker, Hissing Cat, Walks Crooked, North Star, a baby born to us named Carol Sue, and I share the Tee-Pee. We hid in the shadows of the night when the tribe moved. We were unwilling to be one of multiple wives."

150

"So, Michael is not crazy? He actually lived her for three years."

"He was one of us and then he ran away on Road Runner's motorcycle and never returned. Pansy Sky Walker has bore him a child, a girl. I am not fond of the new Weelo child or Pansy. She loves to rub the child in my face. The girl should have been mine and Gray Feather's. He disrespected me giving his child to another. I must look everyday at his disrespect and see that she is fed and cared for. I put her to sleep at night. Pansy Sky Walker, her mother, does not want her and refuses to care for her. I do not want her either, but she is Weelo and I am committed to the survival of my people. I have become the provider for us."

"May I see Gray Feather's child?" he asked in shock never believing that a woman could just come out and say she didn't want a child. How could Moon Dance be so calloused knowing that the girl carried part of Michael in her? This wasn't the loving Moon Dance that his friend had spoken of.

"If you or Pansy Sky Walker do not want her, I will take her home to the Land of New Jersey and raise her as my child. I am a doctor and I will take very good care of her. Michael does not need to know. He would marry Pansy Sky Walker because she is the mother of his child. He dreams of coming home to your arms."

"Follow me and I will show you the child. Watch for snakes and scorpions as we walk. We are short on food and need to catch any meat that might wander our way."

Ralph followed the old woman, who had to be eighty out into the desert and there entered a small camp with one Teepee and several women working and sitting around it. The women were weathered and sat in tattered clothing sharing what looked like a roasted rabbit cooked on a spit on an open fire. They all quickly stood in fear, seeing him.

"Do not fear! This is Ralph Long Legs. He is a medicine man and friend of Gray Feather. All line up. I will spread him a rug to counsel you. He comes with word of Benson."

Ralph sat down on the worn rug the old woman spread for him. He could see the toddler girl, who was a little over two, hiding behind a very old woman who had to be close to a hundred.

"Cross your legs, medicine man. It is the way we do things here. A woman will sit next to you when your legs are crossed and you are then to ask her what she wishes to ask of the Great Spirit."

Ralph did as he was told and crossed his legs. Michael had half way explained to him the counseling ritual when they were standing earlier in the desert where he told of the discarding of his robe and wings.

The first to sit on the rug next to him was the ancient woman who could barely shuffle to his side after giving the hand of the little girl to Moon Dance. With the help of two of the younger women, she sat down on the rug next to Ralph. Her two helpers assisted her crossing her legs for her. She was too old to accomplish it on her own.

When she was seated, Ralph asked "What is your name and what would you ask of the Great Spirit?"

"I am the wife of a great chief. My name is Hissing Cat. I wish to know of Benson. Is he with you as Moon Dance says? He marks the day that the Great Mother Ship will come. I saw it in a dream when I was but a girl of thirteen. My human body is very old and I fear I will cease to be before he and the mother ship arrives. If he is with you, this is a glorious day in the eyes of the Great Spirit and me. I have lived and survived and now will go home. Is Gray Feather with you?"

"This is your glorious day, Hissing Cat. There is a medicine man in the dessert at your spring with Gray Feather named Jack Benson. He will return to the Hogan shortly. He is counseling Gray Feather concerning his lost love and life with Moon Dance." He replied glancing over at Moon Dance who had sadness written all over her face. Michael spoke of a sparkle in her eyes. He didn't see it. Was her heart as shattered as Michael's? Had the light in her soul stopped shining?

"Help me up!" shouted the Old woman named Hissing Cat. The Great Mother Ship is coming today. We must light a moon fire and reflect sun beams so they can find us. We do not have the bullet flyers for communication. I will go to the spring for Benson. I will walk on to the Great Mother Ship with a great medicine man on my arm. I am a chief's wife and I will be respected. Benson was lost in the flood, but now is found. Break up camp, Weelo women. Our days of survival and disrespect are over."

The women helped Hissing Cat to her feet. She held her head high, pushed the women's arms of assistance away, and walked away unassisted for the first time in years toward the spring.

CHAPTER NINETEEN

LONG LEGS DIVORCE

Doctor Ralph Archer was enjoying his experience living his friend Michael's life. He was finding closure walking in his shoes and counseling the tribe for a brief moment in time. He was realizing that Michael had lived a unique experience with people who cared about him during his missing years. He did not have to feel guilty. Michael had been loved.

A young woman sat down who was very beautiful in spite of being weathered and tattered.

Ralph forgot about his two friends. She took his breath away.

"What is your name and what do you wish to ask of the Great Spirit?" he asked.

"My name is North Star. I was married before the men of the tribe left. I do not have the boots of my husband to sit outside the door of my teepee to divorce him. I wish to enter the Great Mother Ship free of him. He has never returned for me or brought me food as he secretly promised me. I now see that his leaving me behind was his way of getting rid of me so that he could take many wives in the Land of Utah that could bear him children. I am barren. I need boots to set out before the ship arrives."

"Do you know what his boots look like in your mind?" Ralph asked.

"Yes, I cleaned them often enough."

"This is a medicine man's prescription pad. I always carry it with me. I will write you a picture of your boots. You will take the magic drawing of the bots into your Tee-pee and then bring the picture of your husband's boots out and place it by your door with a rock on top to hold it down. The rock will keep the magic from blowing away. The rock will make you permanently divorced from him. I, Ralph Long Legs, medicine man to the Weelo speak by the authority of the Great Spirit." He stated really pleased with himself. Michael had told him about the Weelo way of divorcing a man. He could see in the tired eyes of North Star that she needed closure and to be able to move on.

North Star rose to her feet after taking the prescription sheet with drawing on it from him. She broke out into a smile. "I have nothing to pay you with. Would a kiss on the cheek do?"

"I have something better than that to ask of you. I have a wife back home who loves another. I wish to free her to follow her wishes." He stated drawing a quick pair of high heels on one sheet of the pad of prescriptions. I will go with you into the Tee-Pee and out again. I will set my wife's shoes outside the door and divorce her Weelo style. Your payment is to share your rock with me. It will hold your and my divorce in place." He stated and quickly rose to accompany her.

"I like you Ralph Long Legs. Maybe I will take you onto the Great Mother Ship with me. Long Legs and a four o'clock shadow like that of Gray Feather pleases me. Maybe I will take you to the lover's dune if we have time before the Great Mother Ship arrives.

"Let us get these divorces over, North Star. I am willing." He answered seeing something in her eyes that said he had made his way home to the one he had been looking for all of his life. He could see it in her eyes. She was at least ten years younger than him, but it didn't seem to be a problem with her. He was suddenly one happy man. "The Great Spirit and my friend Michael have helped me find my way home to you. I will not climb into a bottle again that I have been lost in."

"You are the one of us in a bottle that I have seen. I am pleased that you have made your way home to me, Ralph Long Legs."

Taking North Star's rough weathered hand in his, they walked into the Tee-pee together and then back out. She placed her paper with drawn boots on the sand by the door. Ralph put his paper with drawn high heels on top of hers. She then went over and scooped up a hot rock up from their fire pit in a handmade small shovel and brought it over and let it fall on top of the two prescription sheets of paper. Instantly, they caught on fire and burned up.

"It is done." Ralph stated taking her hand and interlocking his long fingers in her petite ones. Electricity shot thru him that brought him a feeling of bliss and excitement that he had never known. He had problems performing with Jennifer because he did not love her. There was not going to be a problem with North Star. She had his body's full attention. He blushed. Then he thought of the three children he would have custody of. How would she feel about that? Also, he had asked Moon Dance for Michael's child which would make four.

"It is done." She said squeezing his hand. "Now finish counseling the others. My heart and yours are one. To answer your question, I am barren and want a family. Your children will be my children. I will man one of the Mother ship's flyers when we board the great mother. I am a flyer and I will go for them. I want children and will be a good mother trusting them to no grandfather or uncle. The Captain of the Great Mother will let me bring them on board because they are mine. Usually, we are allowed to bring only one person for passage. Children are the exception."

Ralph squeezed her hand and smiled. "You read my mind."

"I have drawn you here. You are one of us."

"Michael had told him about the Weelo's obsession thinking a great ship is coming for them, a possible Noah's ark." He replied going along with her belief. He would take her home with him to New Jersey tomorrow after their myth was laid to rest.

Ralph sat back down on the rug. He still had two women and one little girl to speak with. A woman slightly older than North Star sat down and crossed her legs. He recognized her as being Pansy Sky Walker from Michael's description. She was equally as tattered and weathered as North Star.

"What is your name and what would you ask of the Great Spirit?" He asked hoping that she didn't know who he was. She had intended to kidnap him, not Michael.

"Benson is the sign pointing us to the coming of the Great Mother. I never believed in the fable till now. I am the tribe story teller, the historian. I have thought that Hissing Cat and Moon Dance were crazy old women. They rescued me from the men of the tribe who intended to hobble me, take me with them, and leave me somewhere in the desert to die. Now, I see that they are indeed leaders of a great people that I have ignored while desiring to be white." She said pausing.

"What is your question?" he asked again.

"I am a half breed. My mother has always told me that Pete Carlson is my father and Connie Carlson is my sister. It has been a great sadness of heart to me that my father has refused to acknowledge me. When I took Gray Feather from the street and brought him here, I honestly thought he was Connie's groom. I wanted something, anything that belonged to my sister. In my mind, I had nothing. I saw her as having everything including my all of my father's love. Taking part of what is rightfully mine has been my obsession. I want to know from the Great Spirit if it is okay for me to go for my father and take him aboard with me.

I can only take one person. Connie hates me."

"If the Great Mother Ship comes today, you will not have time to go for him. I would suggest that you call him and tell him you are sorry for all the pains you have caused him and also your sister. That is the first step in establishing a relationship. Should the Great Mother ship come today, you will have the memory of being respectable and not the thief of Connie's things. Her groom would not have loved you."

"How do you know?" she asked eyeing his dark hair and thinking he looked a lot like Gray Feather.

"I was Connie's groom. I ran in one direction in an angel robe and Michael ran the other drawing the attention away from me so that I could escape. Coming here today, I have found North Star and know with all my heart that she is the other half of me. Had you brought me here, I still would have fallen in love with North Star and not you. She is the other half of me. You cannot have what doesn't belong to you. You cannot make someone love you. You need to wait for that perfect someone to come along."

"It is a little late for that. I have a child that I don't want. I am garbage in the eyes of the Weelo and Gray Feather. He made love to me, but didn't want me after his memory returned. I was shocked to find out that he was not Connie's groom. Connie and I didn't speak for about three years after the wedding event. I had no idea that I had the wrong man. Now it is too late."

"I have asked Moon Dance to let me take Michael's child and raise her. What is her name?"

"Carol Sue." She replied. "That is the only memory Gray Feather ever had. He would have flashes of a great big yellow dog and vaguely remember the name Carol Sue."

"It is a good name. I am sure that one day he will be pleased. I am asking you not to tell Michael that he has a child with you. He will marry you out of a sense of obligation. He is an honorable man. However, he will never love you. I will raise your daughter well and give her everything your father hasn't given you."

"She is yours. That will free me from my shame and disrespect as well as not wanting her."

"He told me about his night with you, Pansy Sky Walker. He says you seduced him by putting your hands all over him. You need to tell Moon Dance. If you don't, she and Gray Feather will not find their way back to each other and both will live and die unloved."

"Moon Dance and I are at odds with each other. She saw Gray Feather making love to me and believes he never loved her. She will not listen to me. She believes that a man that loves you would never look at or consider another. He made love to me and then abandoned me and her. He could have grabbed either one of us and escaped into the desert. Somewhere in his fog and then the clearing of it, he chose another. Grandmother Moon Dance knows and so do I. It is neither of us that Gray Feather dreams of."

"Do it for your daughter if nothing else and a chance to give her a better life. "

Pansy Sky Walker rose from the rug. Take her when you go. I never wish to see her again. Rename her if you wish. I regret the day I took Gray Feather from the street in Bullhorn, Texas. The ship will come and I will not take the child with me. She can die in the desert should you not take her. She is human and worthless the same as I. Moon Dance will take me on board because I am a walking book and the ship's log of our survival as a race. The child has nothing to offer the pure Weelo."

There were only two women left for counseling. Moon Dance picked up the toddler girl named Carol Sue and sat her next to Ralph. Ralph looked into her eyes and instantly fell in love with her. She was his, more so than his own natural children, because he was choosing to father her. A chosen child is a loved child. He was going to make sure that she was spoiled rotten. He owed it to Michael. Also, he was a vet and would never let any dog, cat, or child be harmed if he could help it. These women were withholding love from Carol Sue. He had plenty of it to share with her.

"My name is Ralph Long Legs. Do you have a question for the Great Spirit?" he asked smiling gently at her needing to bond with her."

"Ask my name." she replied giggling.

"Forgive me, what is your name?"

"My name will be whatever yours is!" She giggled." I heard Pansy Sky Walker give me to you."

"I will love you and buy you lots of candy, dolls, and braces for your teeth." He said eyeing her.

"What are candy, dolls, and braces?"

Then it dawned on Ralph that Michael's child had never tasted candy, seen a doll, or had any conception of what medical or dental care were. A tear rolled down his cheek. The animals in his vet clinic had received better care than her.

She was lucky to be alive having been born and living in the harsh existence he was seeing. She had probably never had a toy.

"Candy is sweet food. Dolls are sticks carved to look like little girls like you. Braces are things they put on your teeth to make them grow straight."

"Oh . . ." she replied. "You will be a father who will feed me wild honey, make me sleep with a stick, and force me to smile right."

"You are right. I will be a daddy who will feed you honey, let you sleep with a stick doll of your choice, and make sure that your soul is always shining and your teeth pretty to smile with." He replied grinning and pulling a plastic box of breath mints from his shirt pocket and shaking her one out and one for him. He showed her to put it in her mouth by putting one in his own.

"It stings like a snake and is sweet like honey." She stated big eyed.

"I will always keep the snake sting honey pieces in my pocket for you." He replied. "I will also buy you a doll and something good to eat as soon as we leave here. You will never be hungry or want for anything as long as I have anything to say about it. Whatever is in my pockets is yours. Is there something that you would like to have?"

"Could we forget the honey, the doll, and the smiling teeth? I would just like you to hold me and tell me every day you want and love me. No one here does, except North Star. I am lonely for a father to love me. I am willing to be your dog. Medicine men like dogs."

Ralph picked her up and sat her down on his lap and put his arms around her and stroked her head. "Do you like your head scratched?"

"I am your dog. Yes, you may scratch my head. I will be a good dog. However, I am a girl and would rather have kisses on top of my head and on my cheeks."

Ralph took the hint and then tickled her and kissed her all over her face and neck teasing her. "Maybe I am a great big yellow dog who has found the most wonderful little girl in the world to lick. Licking is how a dog kisses. Maybe I will lick both sides of your face, cheeks, and chin. You won't even have to wash your face before you go to bed. This dog will do it for you."

She squealed and pushed away from him giggling. "I am going to have to train my new father who is a big yellow dog. Do you have fleas?"

Ralph laughed totally amused and in love with her.

Moon Dance took the little girl by the arm and told her to run play so the medicine man could finish his counseling of the women of the tribe. She left, but reluctantly. Ralph was the only visitor and playmate she had ever had.

Moon Dance sat down slowly on the rug and crossed her legs.

"Do you have a question for the Spirit?" he asked already knowing her name.

"I have listened to your counseling. You are a good man. I wish you could help me, but I am beyond help. I loved a man foolishly. I should have known better. I am an old fool who chased a young fart with a brain fog and I have paid. I am ashamed that I loved him and that I hate his child that he gave to another. Do you have a medicine bag to cure old fart men and women? I will be leaving on the Great Mother Ship and not returning. I don't want my heart crying when I am light years from here. I have cried tears from a shattered heart for three years. Being an old fool is a hard thing. I lost my dignity when I watched him in the arms of another making love."

"The medicine bag you need is to have a talk with Gray Feather. He feels like a young fool and has lost his respect and dignity. If there is any magic left between you, it will never be put out. He was wrong to sleep with Pansy Sky Walker. However, he is human and not Weelo like you. Humans are not perfect and they make mistakes. Carol Sue is a mistake. Pansy is correcting her mistake by giving the child to me to rear. I will love and raise her well. I will never tell Michael and she will not interfere in your life anymore. I love kids and want her. You must decide whether you want Michael. He is human and makes mistakes."

"I have considered that he is human. I am pure Weelo and must judge all who come here by Weelo standards. He disrespected me. I do not wish to see him."

"I am sorry, Moon Dance. I can see in your eyes that your spark has died."

"The Lantern of my soul is shattered. Gray Feather put my light out."

CHAPTER TWENTY

A NEW CHIEF

Meanwhile, on the path to the spring in the desert, Hissing Cat screamed like there was no tomorrow when she spotted Gray Feather. She then proceeded to jump up and down a couple times like a giddy school girl and then took off running across the sand pulling energy from somewhere inside her hundred year old body.

Michael was leading the way back to camp keeping an eye out for snakes and scorpions. Jack Benson was following giving the morning and Michael's delusions some serious medical thought. He was also psychoanalyzing himself for having bought into Michael's craziness. He had believed that Moon Dance was real. At night, he dreamed of her and all the events Michael spoke of. After this trip, he was going to insist that Michael see another doctor. He looked up when he heard a woman's screams.

"Hissing Cat . . . ," Michael yelled and started running towards her. He threw his arms around her and held her like there was no tomorrow lifting her up off the desert floor. Nuzzling his head to hers, he burst into tears and so did she. As he cried into the top of her braided hair he said. "I am so sorry for the wasted three years I spent chasing Moon Dance and Pansy. When I stood by the spring remembering, I saw you braiding my hair and the bowl of hot rabbit stew you fed me. I have not forgotten your allegiance to me."

"You have come home, Gray Feather. That is all that matters. I have spent many moons dreaming of your return and that of Benson. Do you now remember that you are a great chief?"

"It all came back to me when I stood at the spring, memories of those who stood by me. A Weelo chief knows who the members of his true tribe are. You are number one with me as well as North Star, Running Deer, and a few others. I have come home to silver bullet lodge, if you will have me?" He said releasing her.

"You are welcome, Gray Feather in my lodge which is now a Tee-pee. You gave yourself to me the day I braided your hair and you ate my rabbit stew. I knew you would one day come home. I was once married to a great human chief. I know a chief when I see one. You are an honorable man."

"I am Weelo and I live and breathe Weelo. Three Toes once sat on my sitter's rug and explained what it was to be a great chief. Now, I honor him and you."

"I have met your friend Ralph. He is one of us, but does not realize it yet. He is still cloudy of the mind from the bottle he has crawled out of. North Star has drawn him to us. Moon Dance has named him Ralph Long Legs. He was not fond of the rattler she caught for dinner. Ralph Long Legs is not a brave medicine man like you. Her snake made him jump and run like a girl."

"He is a little squeamish when it comes to some things." Michael laughed.

About that time, the tribe of women joined Hissing cat and Michael on the path thru the desert that led to the spring.

Ralph, seeing Hissing Cat holding Michael's arm, grinned and gave him the thumbs up. He wanted Michael's homecoming to be a good experience. He was surprised to see someone besides Moon Dance celebrating his return. Moon Dance did not follow the others down the road to the spring.

"This is Hissing Cat." Michael stated with a grin across his face. She is a great chief's wife and much respected. She has welcomed me home to her lodge for a hair braiding and a warming."

"A warming?" Ralph asked in a confused tone.

"When the desert nights get cold, you can sleep next to a Weelo and warm your feet on them if you belong to her. I belong to Hissing Cat. She claimed me when Moon Dance threw me out."

"Hissing Cat owns you?" Ralph asked in total confusion. He was under the impression that Michael had come home to Moon Dance. His friend hadn't mentioned being owned by anyone. In the shock of the moment, he forgot about North Star and his on the spot commitment to her.

The younger women of the tribe helped Hissing Cat to sit down on the desert sand. She was a hundred years old.

"Everyone be quiet." Gray Feather half shouted. "I have something to say."

The dozen or so women became quiet. Gray Feather eyed all of them knowing who his friends truly were. He also saw that Moon Dance was missing from the group. That saddened him, but he knew it was time to move on. The running season of the heart had returned to him just as Hissing Cat had predicted. His winter of the wilted flower bud was over. It was time to love again.

"I am sorry that I have not made my way home sooner. I know longer have a blank slate mind. I know who I once was as well as who I am now. I am not sure why the men of the tribe have abandoned you. However, I am here and I am claiming the position of chief of this tribe. I am Gray Feather and next in line to Three Toes. As chief, I must take a wife. I have considered all of you that stood by me when Moon Dance threw me out and the tribe discarded me. I am back for those of you that showed me allegiance. Any of you would have made a great chief's wife. However, there is respect to consider and the way of the Weelo comes first. As chief, I am taking Hissing Cat as my wife and give her the shoes I have on to place beneath her sleeping blanket. I will love no other. Are you willing Hissing Cat to let me warm my feet on you, now and forever?"

Ralph and Jack Benson both gasped. They hadn't seen this one coming. What happened to his love for Moon Dance?

Suddenly, a very smiling hundred year old Hissing Cat who was sitting on the sand yelled, "Help me up girls, I just won the lottery."

Michael Grinned and helped the younger women to lift and stand Hissing Cat at his side. He then stooped, untied his tennis shoes, took them off and stood holding them in the sky for all to see.

After a moment or two of silence, Michael said, "With this pair of shoes which will have to be considered boots, I now wed Hissing Cat. I will be faithful to her thru eternity and walk with her on my arm onto the Great Mother Ship with honor." Then he lowered the tennis shoes and handed them to Hissing Cat who looked into Gray Feather's eyes biting her lip and grinning. She saw a true Weelo, an honorable man.

Then, it was her turn to speak. Wedding ceremonies amongst the Weelo were simple and sometimes spur of the moment acts.

"Gray Feather, there is something I wish to make very clear to you. Your hissing snake will sleep only in my bed. I realize you are human and that you make mistakes. I will not throw you out. Knowing that I am the stronger of the two of us and pure Weelo, I will wear the pants in our family. You may wear the chief's feathers. As the keeper of you and your hissing snake, I will be fair with you and love you forever."

"My hissing snake is yours and only yours. I, Gray Feather and new chief of the Weelo tribe of women, now take Hissing Cat for my wife." With that said he kissed the hundred year old woman passionately and put one hand on her backside which was a Weelo sign of respect and loving the one you married.

When the kiss was over, Michael spoke. "I know some of you from the Land of New Jersey and those of my tribe do not understand my choice of Hissing Cat. She is older in Earth years than me. The bodies the Weelo live in are not who the Weelo are. I realized it the night I fled the camp. It was Hissing Cat that was there for me in my bad time. It is her that I have returned to. A great chief knows his tribe. I know all of you. Hissing Cat is a woman of great honor, a chief's wife. She has earned her place in my heart by her loyalty to me. I will love no other."

There was a round of hugging and slapping Michael on the back. His two friends were really happy for him although they were aghast thinking of his choice for a wife. She was at death's door in their opinion. They also weren't quite sure of why he had suddenly turned from Moon Dance. They had many questions, but for now, they would not ask them. This was their friend's wedding day.

Jack Benson leaned in to Ralph's space and whispered. "In case you are getting any ideas, Moon Dance is mine. I have been dreaming of her every since Michael returned to us. I think we might have had been a couple thousands of years ago. In my dreams she calls me Noah."

"Have you gone nuts, like Michael?"

Ralph then picked up two plus year old Carol Sue and didn't let her out of his sight. He wasn't sure that there wasn't some sort of crazy bug or virus that was going around. Holding Carol Sue to protect her, he noticed that she had three deformed big toes on one of her tiny feet. He would see to it that she had the surgery needed to remove two of them.

Then it was Hissing Cat's turn to speak when everyone became quiet again.

"There is a great secret of the Weelo that I am going to share with you because the Great Mother Ship is coming today for me. Step a few back from me and watch closely." She stated.

The three men backed up a few feet not knowing what she was up to. Suddenly she pointed her long fingernail on her right hand to the parted area of her braids on top of her head.

"I have worn this Earth Body for a hundred years. I am ready to lay it down because I no longer need to hide amongst the human race. This is the real me." She stated and quickly moved her nail down the center of her face and down the front of her body. Instantly, her Earth body known as Hissing Cat fell limp to the floor like it was a discarded nylon stocking. Out stepped a beautiful woman in a silver jumpsuit and she had skin that was sky blue and eyes of brown. Her hair was pulled up on the top of her head and secured in a silver mesh cap. Long crystal like drop ear jewelry hung dangling and reflecting the desert sun.

The mouths of the three men dropped open in unison because she was so beautiful. She had two oddities. She had three eyes and her ears were crystal. She was an exotic being and definitely not an Earth human. She had two eyes like humans and a third eye in the middle of her forehead that seemed like it could look thru them.

"Are you Hissing Cat, my wife? Am I hallucinating?" Gray Feather asked walking up to the most gorgeous woman he had ever laid eyes on. Only her eyes said she was Hissing Cat.

"I am the chosen new half of your heart, Gray Feather. I have taken off my Halloween face. Are you pleased?"

Michael took her in his arms and kissed her passionately. He let his hands explore his bride ignoring Ralph and Jack. It was his wedding day and his heart and hands were running.

After a few minutes, Jack Benson cleared his throat, "Ahem . . ."

Reluctantly, Michael let his new bride go. He turned to acknowledge his friends. He had one thing on his mind and that was making love to her. Spring had definitely arrived once more for him.

Hissing Cat stepped in front of Michael and spoke.

"The Great Mother Ship from the Planet Weelo is minutes from coming for me and you who stand here. There was once a great happy hunting ground in the sky, a planet that my people traveled to and harvested animals and plants. Thousands of years ago, I arrived here with Moon Dance, North Star, Three Toes, Benson, and Running Deer. We were the main crew of the great ship the white men call Noah's Ark. We were gathering animals to stock our planet when we accidentally dropped an explosive device into the ocean. It caused waves and a flood. Our Great Mother Ship, Noah I, crashed on a mountain blinded by unbelievable sheets of rain. We the crew, managed to save twelve bullet shaped space flyers. We have protected the flyers because it is our only way to enter the mother ship when it comes. We must fly up to it. The women here with Moon Dance and I stole one of the flyers and we have it hidden beneath the sand of the lover's dune. All women here will be granted boarding passes whether they are human or not for their faithfulness and belief. Moon Dance and three of our women are now sweeping the sand from the flyer. North Star is our pilot. We have had to hide in many human bodies and live many human lives. We have done what we have needed to do to survive. I am Hissing Cat Haven. I once was the daughter of the captain of the Great Mother Ship called Noah I. As a child, I pushed the button that dropped the explosive device that caused the Great Flood of Noah. I am sure that I am going to be in big trouble today when I board today. I am probably going to need Gray Feather's shoulder to cry on. Gray Feather is human, but he has earned his place as our chief. He will board with me. Benson has made his way to us. He was once our communications officer. We see and communicate by the mind. He is going home today. It is a glorious day to be alive and know that we have survived the savage of centuries in our wait. During the great flood, some of our people were washed overboard without communication chips and bullet flyers. We have pulled them to us for the Great Ships arrival. Our Great sorrow is that Three Toes and Running Deer are dead. Three Toes died nine months after the Hogan fire from heart failure. Running Deer went off a mountain in her truck in the North also at nine months after the night of the fire. Our original crew has dwindled from one hundred and eighty-two to the handful you see here. Illness and the lack of baby bodies to step into, has brought about the death of ninety percent of us. We the Weelo have survived planet Earth and its human race. Now we are going home. Each true Weelo may take one human with him. Choose wisely. Carol Sue has chosen her new father, Ralph Long Legs."

Ralph kissed Carol Sue affectionately on top of her head. He loved his new raven haired, brown eyed pet. He scratched her on her head to annoy her. Then he stood her down on the ground next to him and held securely to her hand. He knew there had to be rattlers everywhere. He would be glad when he got her back to New Jersey where it was safe.

About that time, a great gray cloud appeared and started lowering itself in the atmosphere. All present shielded their eyes with their hands and stared. A great Space Craft the size of ten foot ball fields descended and hovered a couple miles above the Earth's surface blocking the noon day sun.

"Oh my God," Ralph said turning to Jack Benson. He hadn't bought into the Great Mother Ship thing. "No wonder we couldn't find Michael when he disappeared. "He was abducted by aliens!"

Then, Doctor Ralph Archer fainted.

Three doctors disappeared that day in the desert of New Mexico, as well as three young children and one golden Collie from the land of New Jersey.

"Alien Encounters"

a Three Book Series by Jo Hammers

GRAY FEATHER'S FOG
Book One now available

MOON DANCE
Book two available July I, 2012

PANSY'S REVENGE
Book three in 2013

Made in the USA
Monee, IL
10 February 2021